Beauty and the Beast Retold

CURSE of the Taniwha

CATHERINE MEDE

FLYING KIWI
PRESS

Curse of the Taniwha

Amazon ISBN 978-0-473-51747-2

pdf ISBN 978-0-473-51748-9 -

Paperback ISBN 978-0-473-51745-8

This book is dedicated to

anyone who loves

Beauty and the Beast

Chapter 1

RENA DROPPED HER PACK onto the tussock-covered ground. She stripped off her long-sleeved shirt, tied it around her waist and wiped the back of her hand across her forehead. She stretched out her shoulders before reaching for the drink bottle clipped to the side of her pack. She took a big gulp of water. The cool liquid, sliding down her parched throat, quenching her thirst, tasted so good. She reattached the bottle and executed a couple of yoga stretches before scooping her shoulder-length dark blonde hair into a ponytail. Using the elastic band twined around her left wrist, she secured it. The slight breeze caressing her naked neck cooled her down. She lifted her arms above her head and felt the stretch work the muscles in her back. A sigh escaped her as she hoisted the heavy pack onto her shoulders.

She settled the weight against her spine and surveyed the surrounding countryside. No cars, no houses, no civilisation. Only the sounds of nature surrounded her; the breeze whispering through the stringy grass, the birds chirping in the nearby bush.

Compared to the hustle and bustle of the city, this was silence.

Peace.

A setting she loved.

She shifted the pack into a more comfortable position and set off towards the Sabine hut in Nelson Lakes National Park.

Rena Collings would have preferred to spend all her time in the outdoors. Sitting at a desk all day was her idea of hell. But she needed to pay the bills somehow, and if she could get out into the wilderness from time to time, she was happy.

She'd set off early from Angelus, after noting in the hut's book her intention to head towards Sabine and stay there for the night. The trek was long and mostly downhill on a steep gradient.

The bush line beckoned, and she entered the cool darkness provided by the high canopy, enjoying a respite from the heat of the summer sun. The area would be lovely to tramp in during wintertime, although then, snow would cover most of the track, making it harder and slower to walk. Even in the summertime, pockets of snow turned to crystallised ice still marked the landscape.

As she came down towards Lake Rotoroa, the track, slick with dead leaves, steepened and she slipped. Her hands shot out and grabbed for the surrounding foliage. A tumble off the track could be the end of her. She stopped, waiting for her racing heart to slow before she took another step.

With adrenalin rushing through her veins, she picked a path along a particularly steep section. Despite her caution, she skidded across the slippery surface and landed on her bottom at the edge of the trail. Stunned, she sat for a moment to gather her bearings. Then, moving her feet underneath her, she lurched to a stand. The earth crumbled away beneath her. She screamed and desperately grappled for a hold, something to keep her from slipping further down the bank. But the weight of her pack proved too much, toppling her backwards, and she fell down the slope. Branches and sharp stones tore at her hair, skin and clothes as she tumbled through the bush. Her head bounced off a rock, knocking her half senseless. Her body rolled on. She came to a halt against a couple of trees.

Pain scrambled her thoughts.

Everything aches so badly.
Too badly. Just rest for a moment.
Catch your breath.

She closed her eyes, willing her spinning head to catch up with her body. A few minutes passed before the pounding in her head took over, causing a bout of dizziness and nausea to wash through her. Ignoring the giddiness, she took a deep breath.

She lay awkwardly. Her pack was trapped beneath her, holding her up in a semi-seated position. Nerves zapping along her spinal cord caused a tingling in her back and her legs felt like she'd run a marathon. She tried to push herself up but couldn't alter her position. When she attempted to move her legs, one refused while the shaft of pain shooting through the other halted her efforts. She looked down at her torn leggings. A bone protruded from the front of her right leg. Nausea roiled her stomach.

She swallowed back the bile that surged up her throat and reached for her water container. Although a little battered, the flask had survived the fall.

She swallowed a little water and then, gathering her strength, yelled at the top of her voice, "Help!"

The bird call quietened, and she caught the sound of a splash. She wasn't far from the lake. Wedged between the trees by her pack, she couldn't look in that direction. Neither could she see the track up above, only the broken branches and scrape marks marking the path of her fall. She lay her head against her pack, her back arching unnaturally. A tear slid from beneath her closed lids as the stabbing pain settled into a constant throb.

"Help!" she called again.

Then she remembered. Her pack contained a personal locator beacon. She struggled to free her arms from the straps holding her prisoner, but they clasped her tightly, allowing no escape. Sobbing at the futility of her efforts, she gave up.

To stop herself from screaming, she picked up the flask and sipped more water. As the adrenalin wore off, the pain would increase. She needed to keep a calm head.

She exhaled and took several deep breaths.

You can do this Rena; you can get up.

If she could get her legs underneath her, she could stand. Pushing down on her hands, she tried to pull her legs up towards her chest, but her broken leg wouldn't respond.

Searing pain flooding her senses, and she cried out.

She took a moment to gather her courage and she tried again. Panting, she pushed up once more, determined to move. This time, the explosion of pain ended in darkness.

-oOo-

Rena opened her eyes. She lifted her head and gazed at her surroundings. Memories rushed in and she moaned. She was trapped in the bush with a broken leg. Heart pounding, she glanced up. The sun had moved. No longer was it directly overhead. Her watch showed late afternoon. Cool air trickled in around her. Although the middle of summer, she was at a high altitude. Nights got cold up there. Her eyes blurred, and she blinked to clear them.

"Relax." The smooth, gruff voice took her unawares.

She flipped her head from side to side but couldn't see anyone. "Who are you? Where are you?"

"Behind you. Just relax."

She tried to look over her shoulder. "Get me out of here!" Pain and fear laced her voice with desperation and the words came out in a screech.

"I'm doing all I can."

"My leg is broken."

"I can see that."

A figure moved into her field of vision, but she couldn't distinguish any features through her blurred vision. She squinted, but all she could make out was that a tall and thickly-built man in green stood over her legs, holding what appeared to be two long sticks in his hand.

"This is going to hurt," said his smooth voice, quieter than normal. He blew out a breath and worked to place one stick either side of the broken limb and, using what she recognised to be the thermal top she'd earlier tied around her waist, he pulled her leg straight and bound it to the splints.

She screamed before the darkness swamped her, once again.

-oOo-

Pitch black greeted her when she woke up. The pain had receded to a dull ache, and she was warm.

How could that be?

She remembered the stranger. "Hello?" she called into the night.

"You're awake then?" That voice. She could fall in love with that deep and husky voice. Smooth like silk and rich like chocolate. A total romance lover's dream.

"I ... I think so." She attempted a smile, but her lips refused to obey. Her body ached so badly. She wriggled, expecting some restriction to the movement, but the pack was gone from behind her.

"Where am I?"

"Near Lake Rotoroa."

"Oh!" She wondered why she was still there.

A crinkling noise accompanied her move to sit up. The silver blanket he'd placed over her glinted in the faint light filtering through the trees.

"I have set off your beacon. Help should be here soon. Probably not until morning, though."

"Can't you get me out of here?" she asked.

"No, I can't move you."

'Why not?" Her voice pitched as she tried to twist around to look at the person.

"Your leg is too badly broken."

She sat in silence. Even her basic first aid training said you shouldn't move a patient who could have spinal or neck injuries. Her injuries were less serious, but this guy didn't know that. She could sense the man sitting beside her but, in the darkness, she could make out little of his features, other than that he was large, both in stature and height.

"What's your name?" Silence greeted her query. Nothing moved, not even the shadow beside her.

"I'm thirsty," she murmured.

"Here, drink this." He offered Rena her own canteen, but the water tasted different; colder, more refreshing.

"What is this?"

"You drank the last of your water, so I refilled your flask from the spring."

"What spring?"

"Don't worry, it won't hurt you. Just drink it."

She hesitated, then drank the water, which didn't taste too bad once she'd swallowed it.

"I'm hungry, do you have anything to eat?"

"No, I'm afraid not."

"There might be something in my bag."

"I did find something when I looked through it earlier," he said.

"You went through my pack?"

"I had to keep you warm, didn't I?"

"Why not a fire?"

A growl erupted from the stranger's throat. "I don't light fires."

"Then how do you keep warm?"

Again, he didn't answer her question. He shuffled through her pack, and then said in a gruff voice, "Here."

She peered at the object dangling inches from her face. "How about a light or something?"

"I don't have a torch."

"There's a flashlight in my pack," she said, softening her tone.

"It's smashed."

He placed the bar in her palm. She curled her fingers over the treat, touching the stranger's hand. His skin was smooth, but cold to the touch.

"Are you from around here?" she asked to make conversation. While she liked quiet, the darkness and pain overwhelmed her mind, and she needed the comfort of another human voice.

"I live locally."

"Where?" She bit a chunk off the health bar.

"Around." She pursed her lips and narrowed her eyes.

She munched on the bar, savouring the taste in her mouth, aware of his presence and his size. Although he was hunkered down beside her, she could judge his height by the location of his voice.

Bird calls slowly awakened the darkened forest.

"First light. Help will be here soon," he mumbled. He seemed to be getting up.

"You aren't leaving me, are you?" Her heart hammered against her chest.

"I have to go. Help will arrive soon. You'll be all right."

"But what if I need more help before they arrive?"

"You have plenty of water in your canteen and another bar beside you, you'll be fine." Heavy footsteps crashing through the undergrowth indicated he was leaving.

"Please?" she called out. But no response came; only the fading sound of his departure and the increasing call of the birds as daylight chased away the darkness.

"I didn't even get to say thank you," she muttered. She lay back down, warm under her blanket, and dozed off.

Chapter 2

BUZZING INTERRUPTED HER WARPED dreams, waking her. Shouting voices came from above and below her.

"Over here!" she called.

"Rena? Ms Collings? Is that you?"

"Yes, I'm down the bank." High up above her, a head popped over the edge of the track. She'd fallen from higher up than she'd thought.

"Are you all right?"

"No, I have a broken leg and I can't move."

"Just hold on while I radio your position to the boat. They'll get you out."

A whistle and tinny voices drifted on the air, and then sounds of a boat's motor in the distance, the drone becoming louder as it came towards her. Although lying down, she could see through gaps between the bushes. A white runabout was approaching her position. She waved her arm and called out to them.

"Ms Collings?" The voice sounded concerned. The boat's motor cut out and was instantly replaced by sounds of splashing.

"Yes, I'm up here." She waved to the shadow that moved into the bush. His dark face turned towards her, and his eyes brightened. A big grin lit up his face as he raced up the small embankment to get to her. Her heart leapt at the sight of him.

He was handsome.

Her knight in shining armour was like a storybook hero.

"Are you okay, Ms Collings?"

"Please, call me Rena," she said, dipping her head and looking through her eyelashes at the gorgeous stranger with honey brown eyes. "I slipped on the track."

"Rob," he said, holding out a hand. She slipped her own into his warm grasp and, with exaggerated gentleness, he pumped it.

His eyes travelled the length of her, as if assessing the situation.

"I broke my leg."

"How badly?" he asked, kneeling beside her and lifting the blanket. His olive skin blanched. "It's really hard to break that bone. You did a number on it though, didn't you!" He scrambled to his feet.

"Can we get out of here? I'm cold, damp and tired. I just want to rest."

"No problem, Ms Collings." He turned and grinned at her, his teeth flashing white and his dark eyes lightening. She smiled back, pushing an errant strand of hair behind her ear. He patted her hand, lingering over it longer than necessary. She resisted the urge to sigh. He was handsome, caring *and* gentle.

Splashing behind him indicated more men were on their way. She spied one carrying a back board.

"The ride home isn't going to be easy, but there'll be a chopper ride. Don't worry Ms Coll ... Rena, we'll have you better in no time."

"What about the other guy?"

"What other guy? Is there another person hurt?" He turned to head back into the bush, but she stopped him.

"There was a man here. He helped me. He set off the beacon." He looked around, confusion clouding his face.

"No one else is out here, Rena. No one else is on the track."

"But ... the man, he made me comfortable, gave me water, he helped me..." Her voice faltered at the expressions on the faces of the rescue team who congregated around her. One knelt and felt her forehead, another took her pulse.

"Are you sure you weren't hallucinating?"

"I wasn't hallucinating." She clamped her jaw shut; she knew better than to keep talking. They all thought she was delusional.

Someone placed a neck brace in Rob's hand. He knelt and, pulling her ponytail aside, slid it around her neck.

"I don't have any neck injuries," she grumbled, her ears and cheeks heating up at Rob's closeness.

He patted her shoulder. Two men moved the back board in beside her. She knew before Rob spoke what he was going to say.

"I'm not going to lie. This is going to hurt." Rob squeezed her hand. The three men lifted her up onto the hard board. Her scream echoed across the lake. Once they had her settled, they strapped her onto the board, keeping her body still and her neck stiff under the band that went across her forehead.

"Will you stay with me?" she asked Rob. She couldn't turn her neck to see him, but he moved into view, smiled down at her, and pushed a curl over her ear. The touch zapped her like an electrical shock.

"Anything for you," he said. He smiled and his eyes sparkled.

Heat rushed up her neck and into her face. She closed her eyes.

-o0o-

The helicopter lowered onto the helipad at Nelson Hospital. The descent made her giddy, never mind the painkillers they had given her. A drip leaked fluid into her arm, and the pain had eased back to a dull ache.

True to his word, Rob stayed with her all the way. She'd learnt he was a Department of Conversation officer working at the Lake Rotoiti office. He told her off for not having the locator beacon on her person. Putting it in her pack had been a silly mistake, but not one she would repeat.

"Here you are, Ms Collings. We will hand you over to the ED staff now," said the paramedic who'd accompanied them in the helicopter. The stretcher was wheeled out of the chopper, in through the side door of the hospital and into a busy Emergency Department. Rooms were partitioned off, and groans and crying came from some of them. The strong smell of bleach filled her nostrils, and she almost threw up. The smells and sounds were overwhelming.

"Are you all right, Rena? You look pale," Rob asked, stroking curls off her clammy forehead.

"I don't feel so good."

The orderly quickly pushed her stretcher into a bay and called for a nurse. The nurse looked her over and put a hand on Rena's forehead. The cool hand reduced her panic and heat slowly suffused back into her face. The nurse bustled about the bed, putting on a blood-pressure cuff, checking her temperature, testing her eye reaction. She seemed satisfied and smiled kindly at Rena.

"A doctor will see you shortly," she said.

Rena sighed. That could mean any time during the next three hours.

"It'll be all right," Rob said, rubbing her good leg.

Rena grimaced.

"Does that hurt?"

"No, it feels strange."

"Sorry."

"No need to be sorry, just feels weird because the other leg has a bone poking out of it in nearly the same place. I guess the left leg is going out in sympathy."

Rob laughed. "I know what you mean." He looked up, and their eyes caught and held. Rena thought she could see into Rob's soul, and she liked what she saw. A handsome man, a hero no less, who worked in the great outdoors.

He enjoyed hunting and tramping.

And he was single. He'd told her that earlier, after she'd told him she had no significant other.

He leaned forward, his eyes never leaving hers, and his lips softly brushed her own. A zap of energy travelled down her spine and settled in her lower stomach. She leaned towards him, opening her mouth under his, allowing his tongue to explore.

As the kiss was about to deepen, the curtain slid back, and the doctor arrived, followed by Sharna, who Rena had called once they'd gotten within cell phone range.

"My god girl, what have you been doing to yourself?" Sharna bustled her way over to Rena and smothered her in a perfume-shrouded hug. Rena reached out her hand toward her best friend.

"Oh, you know, just throwing myself down a bank."

"That was stupid."

"Wasn't the cleverest thing I've done."

"Ahem."

Rena shifted her gaze to the man in the white coat.

"Ms Collings? I'm Doctor Roger Petherbridge. We will be sending you through for X-rays. Although we know your left tibia is broken, we need to make sure nothing else is damaged, plus we need to check that head of yours. I understand you passed out immediately after the fall?"

"Yes, I did."

"Okay. Well, here is the form, and the orderly will take you through shortly."

"Thank you, Doctor," Rena said. Sharna fake swooned as he left the room and mouthed, "He's hot" as she fanned herself with one hand. That was Sharna – always chasing after stunningly handsome, unavailable men.

"Get a grip, Sharna," Rena said, laughing. Her friend turned around and spotted Rob, who'd pressed himself up against the wall.

"And who is this young stud muffin?"

Rob face turned a bright brilliant red.

Heat flooded Rena's cheeks and she hissed in a low voice, "Sharna! This is Rob, he was one of the search and rescue team."

"Hell-o Rob." Sharna sashayed across the room. Rena raised her eyes and glanced at Rob. He smiled.

Sharna batted her long dark eyelashes at him. "Are you seeing anyone?" She glanced over at Rena.

Rob shoved his hands in his pockets and ducked his head. A blush reddened his cheeks.

"Well, I've just started seeing someone." He pulled out his right hand and rubbed it through his short black hair.

Rena's insides froze. Hadn't he told her, not even half an hour ago, he was single? He looked over at her, a wide smile curving his lips and warming his dark eyes, but his expression didn't make her feel any better.

"Oh well, that's no good, big boy. I'm sure she doesn't compare with me?"

"No, possibly not, but I'm willing to find out." He moved towards the bed and took Rena's hand. She tried to pull it out of his grip and winced as his clasp tightened.

"It's you, silly. Will you go out with me?" The words took a while to filter into her brain. He was talking about her. He wanted to go out with her. She stared at him. Mischief glinted in his eyes.

"Well, she's a lucky girl." Sharna's tone took on a cold edge. "Just remember, you hurt her, and I will hunt you down and kill you. Understand Rob?"

Rena laughed, trying to brush off her friend's warning. She wasn't sure she meant the threat. But a glance at Rob's steely face told her he'd taken Sharna's words seriously. The mischievous twinkle had disappeared, replaced by a cool gaze.

A quiet warning whispered in her consciousness, but she ignored it. The look on Rob's face was far more intense than it should be. Rob and Sharna were only playing. He and Rena weren't even in a relationship yet.

Get a grip, girl. She needed to relax and let things happen. At the moment, she couldn't do a hell of a lot, except wait for the radiologist to X-ray her leg.

-oOo-

Two weeks later, Rena, balanced on a pair of crutches, rested at the bottom of the elevator bank waiting for Sharna to bring the car around to the back of the hospital.

Rena was sick of lying inside. She'd been bed-ridden for a week until the infection cleared up in her leg. Then they'd set it in a cast that went from her ankle, with a bend for her knee, and halfway up her thigh. She hated being constricted. But, at least with crutches, she could get outside and enjoy fresh oxygen instead of the hot stale air that permeated the hospital ward. She took a breath as the doors opened to reveal Rob half-hidden behind the large bunch of flowers in his arms. His face lit up. She pushed herself up onto her crutches and moved towards him.

"Hello, doll," he said, kissing her cheek. "They letting you escape for a while?"

"No, I've been given the DCB." Her smile was broad as she glanced up at him, her eyes taking in the flush colouring his cheeks.

"DCB?"

"Don't come back."

Rob's eyes darkened. He took a step back. "They're discharging you. Why didn't you ring and let me know?"

"I tried to, but your phone was off. So, I rang Sharna. She's taking me to her place for a couple of days."

"Sharna's? Why don't you come out to my place instead?" His tone contained a note of pleading, and something else that disturbed her.

"I want to spend some time with Sharna and get the ACC forms sorted out. I'll need physio soon too, for my leg, so I need to be close and handy."

"I can bring you in. How about you stay at Sharna's for a couple of nights and then come out to my place?"

"I could probably do that." Rena grinned at him. He smiled back, but his eyes were looking elsewhere. His body was rigid, and he didn't seem happy. She reached out a hand and took his, but he shook her off.

"And there you are. I was waiting outside for you. Oh, hi Rob." Sharna smiled and winked at him but got no response.

"I'll call you in a couple of days," he said, pushing the flowers into Sharna's arms. He stalked out of the foyer without a backward glance.

"Yep, bye now," Rena said softly. His words had pierced her, but she put it aside. She was going to have a sleepover with her bestie for two nights. Enough time to sort things workwise and complete all the necessary forms.

"Ready to rock and roll?" Sharna's smile brushed away all her fears.

"I don't know about rock and roll, but wobbling or waddling, yeah, I think I can handle that."

The girls laughed. Sharna picked up Rena's overnight bag and slung it over her shoulder and, keeping a motherly eye on her friend, led her from the hospital.

Chapter 3

Six Months Later...

Rena wriggled in her seat trying to get comfortable. Rob was driving her to his property at St Arnaud and her leg ached from being all cramped up in the cab of his utility. Her broken limb had taken longer to heal than expected. That no major infection had set into the bone had caused the doctors some surprise, although they said the poultice they'd found covering the break might have had something to do with preventing toxicity. Not that she remembered putting it there, or anyone else putting it there, for that matter. She had vague recollections of talking with someone, a man with a deep, gravelly voice and smooth hands. Her eyebrows lowered.

Perhaps I dreamed it?

She glanced over at Rob. The road was winding, and he was staring intently out the windscreen. His initial attentiveness had been endearing, except for the incident on the day she was discharged from hospital. He'd called her up two days later, very apologetic, wanting to take her out to his place for the weekend.

For the two weeks she stayed at Sharna's he called her every night, and they spoke for hours about anything and everything. Rena, being confined to the house, loved listening to him talk about his day. He would explain what he'd done, where he'd been, what he'd seen. She would close her eyes and imagine the scene as he described them. Rob asked her if she was okay but didn't ask much else about her day.

After two weeks, he broached the subject of her staying with him for the long weekend.

"I'm coming into town, so I can pick you up and bring you back after the weekend. Does that sound good to you?"

Rena loved Sharna, and she was thankful that she had let her stay with her, but the idea of a weekend away from Nelson sounded enticing.

"I would love it," she said.

When she had told Sharna, she wasn't as happy. "Are you sure you want to go there for a few days?"

"Sharna, I'll be fine."

Sharna put her hands on her hips as she stood in the middle of the lounge. "I don't like him. There is something about him that makes my skin crawl."

"You're just over-reacting because he wasn't into you." Rena laughed, but stopped when she saw the coldness in her friend's eyes. Sharna crossed her arms.

"Remember how he reacted when I picked you up from the hospital?"

"Come on Rena, he had driven all the way in from St Arnaud to see me."

"Yeah, and he could have come around to my place to spend time with you."

"Not with the way you act around him. You probably frightened him off," Rena replied. Her heart plummeted in her chest at her friend's bitterness. She was pleased that she had accepted Rob's invitation. Perhaps she needed a break from her best friend.

The following morning he'd picked her up, promised Sharna she would be fine and, showing awareness of every bump and rock on the road, slowly driven her to his retreat.

They'd both been quiet during the journey. Rena was glad to be away from the bustling town and back in St Arnaud. Rob pulled off the road and stopped in front of a small square house. Not at all what she expected. Tussock grass grew in patches around the property, which was protected by a high wooden fence on three sides. No colourful garden broke the monotony of the earthy tones. He clambered out, opened the gate, and parked the car in a small carport.

Rena waited. He rounded the car and opened the door for her. Leaning in, he cupped her elbow and assisted her gently from the car. She leaned against the warm metal while he retrieved her crutches from the back of the cab. She followed him into the house.

The building was more spacious than she'd first thought, with an open plan lounge, a kitchen, a dining area and two bedrooms upstairs. Rena looked at the stairs and felt defeated. Rob smiled as he laced his arms around her, making her drop the crutches. He picked her up and swept her up the stairs to the master bedroom, a large airy space, containing a large bed, two sets of drawers and a wardrobe with sliding doors. He took her into the en suite. A large bath sunk into the floor provided a view out the window over the valley below.

She gasped at the sight.

They made love that first night, tentatively, gently. Rob had been tender, showing her a side to him that she had never seen in a man before. He was romantic, stroking her body, massaging her muscles, his fingers caressing her back, sides, legs, arms and finally her breasts, stoking her fire for a while before they made love. He didn't want to hurt her, but she didn't want to hurt him by accidently kicking him with her cast. It was damned heavy to manage and would leave a nasty bruise. They lay in a state of bliss and talked into the night of their hopes and dreams for the future, finding a lot in common. She liked the outdoors, he was a conservation ranger. He loved the mountains around, hence the purchase of the old bach, which he had totally gutted and re-insulated, making it a hot house, rather than an ice box in the winter. The gardens were something that needed work, and it was something that Rena was interested in helping him with.

The more they talked, the more Rena felt herself falling for Rob.

Rena enjoyed the peace and tranquillity so much, that Rob easily convinced her to stay. On Monday morning, she rang Sharna.

"I'm staying out here for the week, Sharna. It's so peaceful."

"Are you sure that's the right thing to do?"

"Why do you ask that?"

"Well, you saw his reaction when you came home with me. Are you sure this is your decision and not his?"

"Sharna! Rob has work, and I'm staying for the quiet. It's not like I'm moving in with him. Don't worry, I'll be all right. And I can ring – or better yet, you ring and check on me every night, okay? Does that sound suitable to you?" Rena laughed, but Sharna's silence suggested her friend didn't find it funny.

"I'm fine here, Sharna, I promise. And I'll see you next Sunday. Okay?" she said, reiterating her intentions.

Sharna sighed. "Okay, honey, as long as you know what you are doing." Irritation sharpened her voice.

"This, coming from the woman who's been trying to pair me off with any single man she's come across for the last two years."

"Not every single man!"

"Just about!"

"All right, I will ring you tonight. Just take care."

"Okay, Sharna, I promise."

A few days later, she went back to her flat, packed her meagre belongings and moved some of them out to Rob's place. The rest she put into storage. While off work on the national accident compensation plan, her job position had become redundant. So, with no job to go back to, she had no reason to go back to town. Lake Rotoiti seemed like a tranquil and peaceful place to convalesce.

Rob smiled at her. Five months was a long time. A lot had changed. His eyes, which once sparkled so brightly when he smiled, were now dull, almost angry-looking. "Everything okay?"

She nodded and turned to look out the window at the passing scenery.

They'd been to Nelson Hospital for her check-up and physio appointment. The doctor had removed her cast and seemed pleased that the skin was pink and healthy, and the bone had knit nicely. She no longer needed the crutches or a replacement cast. That the bloody thing was finally off pleased her no end. The inability to move around freely had driven her batty. She was looking forward to a long, hot bath when they got back to Rob's place.

If he let her.

She sighed. An image of her old flat drifted into her mind.

She told her flatmate she was leaving and paid up to date with her rent. She moved in with Rob, and everything was ideal, for a while.

After a couple of weeks, he started to snap at her about little things. The floor not being vacuumed, the dust settling on the television, dinner not being cooked and ready when he got home. The little things started to mount up and before long, Rena felt she was a servant within the home. With no way of escaping the house, she felt trapped.

She didn't want to tell Sharna, because she would just say 'told you so', which she didn't want to hear. She was in touch with Sharna, but the more she spoke about her, the more Rob complained about everything Sharna said, so she stopped talking about her, and slowly stopped contacting her.

She tried harder to make Rob happy, tried to make things better. Vacuumed daily, dusted, cleaned, bleached, and polished every surface, had dinner cooked and ready to go when he got home, but still, it wasn't enough. Even their sex deteriorated to a state of almost rape. He wouldn't take no for an answer, and she felt obligated to give him what he wanted, just to keep him happy.

But the harder she tried; the worse things got.

She was trapped.

She had wanted to stay with Sharna, and she would've been better company, but Rob had work the next day and wanted to get home. He didn't want to drive in and out of St Arnaud to get her, and he'd indicated that Sharna wouldn't be welcome at his house.

A small amount of resentment niggled at her brain.

Rob hadn't encouraged visitors either, saying he preferred only the two of them.

Deep down inside, Rena knew he was isolating her from her friends. She stared at his profile. He couldn't be so cold and calculating, could he? She turned to look out the window again. Thoughts and memories flickered through her mind: comments made, snide comments that she'd brushed off at the time; missed phone calls from friends, who didn't leave messages; the times she could have gone into town and hung out with friends, but Rob would frown and tell her she would tire herself out.

Maybe he is trying to keep me away from my friends?

"Penny for your thoughts?" he asked.

Heat rushed into her face and, not for the first time, she wondered whether he could read her mind.

"Looking forward to getting home and having a bath."

"Uh huh," he said. "And?"

"There is no 'and'."

"Oh, I thought you might've been thinking about what the doctor said."

"The doctor said a lot of things."

"Yes, but he said you shouldn't go out tramping for a while."

Rena's cheeks grew hotter and she ground her teeth. Trust Rob to focus in on *those* words.

"Like I'm going to want to head out on a tramp in the next week!" she spat out.

"Don't take it out on me." His eyes narrowed and his tone was icy.

She shook her head and stared out the passenger window.

Trust him to pick a fight. Rena ignored him for the rest of the ride home. At one point, she turned on the radio, only to have Rob huff and switch it off. She bit back a retort, sat back, and watched the forestry rush by.

An hour is a long time to sit in uncomfortable, icy silence.

-o0o-

Rob's truck pulled up his driveway and under the carport, Rena hopped out of the cab without waiting for him to open her door. Without the crutches to balance her, her gait felt strange, but she waddled inside and straight to the bathroom. She locked the door and turned on the taps, running her bath.

Six months she'd been stuck inside, either in hospital or at Rob's place. He allowed her little time outside, even though she yearned for the sun on her face. Rob said he was concerned about the changing weather, that he didn't want her to catch a chill. She thought it had more to do with the neighbour on the other side; a handsome forestry worker who often spoke to her over the fence. Although their chats consisted of only cordial greetings and discussions about the weather, Rob had seen her talking to him, and called her inside for something. Whenever he saw her talking to someone, he would interrupt and make up some excuse for her to focus her attention back to him.

She glanced in the mirror. Her blonde hair was pulled back and gathered in a ponytail. Pulling off the tie, she allowed it to flow down to rest on her shoulders. She fluffed it out. Her normally bright blue eyes stared back grey and lifeless. She felt drained from the journey into town and the tense standoff in the car. Shifting out here didn't seem like such a good idea anymore.

If she didn't make a move soon, she would be stuck here.

Rob had talked her into staying with him for a year, so she could get herself back on her feet. Another six months seemed a long time. She needed to find her own independence again. Rob had made her dependent on him, and while the thought of going out on her own frightened her, she'd done it for five years before she met him.

Living in a place of her own would help their relationship ... surely?

She turned from the fogged-up mirror, sat on the side of the bath, and trailed her fingers through the steaming water.

Stripped off, Rena eased herself into the water and released a long, loud sigh. She was totally wet, including her skinny leg, and it felt amazing. She picked up the shower gel and soaped her leg, feeling along the limb for any other changes. Muscles had faded to nothing and would take time to build back up. The scar was raised and pink, but other than that – and six months of hair growth – everything felt fine. She shaved her legs, and then lay back, closed her eyes and tried to relax, allowing the heat of the water to calm her fractured nerves.

She climbed out of the bath, dried herself and pulled her dressing robe around her naked body. She let the water out and opened the door as quietly as she could, wanting to get dressed without Rob knowing she was out of the bath because she was sure he would want to have sex. The last thing she wanted right now.

Noises on the lower floor indicated he was in the kitchen area. She scrambled into the bedroom and pulled open the wardrobe doors. She hurried to pull on some panties and a bra. Even the underwear made her feel more comfortable.

She jumped when a pair of arms snaked around her waist.

"You're on edge right now, aren't you?" His smooth voice whispered in her ear.

"Sorry, it's been a long day and I'm tired," she replied, not turning to look at him. She didn't want to look at him. He'd made her angry in the car and calming down took her a while. Unfortunately, Rob still didn't get this about her.

He turned her around to face him, pulled her tight against him and ground his groin into her. She put her hands on his chest and pushed to put some distance between them, but he held her tight. A hard knot formed in her stomach. She gave him a tight smile.

"Too tired for me?" His eyes darkened, and his tone was chilly.

"Yes, too tired for you." She sighed, hoping he would get the hint, but she knew he wouldn't.

"Oh, baby, let me rub your back for you."

An excuse for him to try and get her in the mood. That wasn't what she wanted.

"Not now. I'm hungry."

"Oh. All right then." Casting hurt eyes down, she knew he was pulling the sympathy card on her. He was the travel agent for guilt trips. She broke away from his grip, scrambled for a dress and, after pulling it on, escaped down to the kitchen. Rob showed his disapproval by stomping around the house.

Chapter 4

ALTHOUGH SHE WENT OUT for exercise, slowly strengthening her leg, the days dragged by. She walked around the village and met some of the locals. Something she couldn't do when using crutches because her hands suffered if she travelled too far. Now though, she was able to make new friends. Not that many were friendly, especially if she mentioned Rob's name. Most of them smiled, nodded, and then found other jobs to do. No one spoke or asked after the man, which she thought was unusual. Rob had warned that some locals were nasty gossips and only said bad things about him, but she hadn't heard anything. However, that they avoided talking to her made her wonder if perhaps he was right.

"Why would they say nasty things about you?" Rena asked Rob one day.

His shoulders hitched closer to his ears. "They will make things up regardless. Like I'm a woman-beater, or woman-hater," he said, not looking up from the paper he was reading.

"I haven't heard that one."

"Well, you know differently, don't you?"

"And I could convince them too."

He huffed, put the paper down and stared at her. "I don't care, just don't talk to people, okay?"

"I guess."

"What do you mean 'I guess'?" He got up and came over to her. Then he grabbed her shoulders, his fingers pinching her skin.

"I just meant that I won't talk to people. Ow, Rob, you're hurting me."

He let go of her shoulders and rubbed them.

"I'm sorry. I didn't mean to." The smile didn't reach his eyes. He was trying to soothe her, but he wasn't succeeding, only setting her nerves on edge.

Since the cast had been removed his behaviour had changed. His temper was shorter, and he often came home from work moody.

-oOo-

After two weeks of recuperation, she spent her days walking some of the trails around Lake Rotoiti: Honeydew Track, Bellbird Track, Peninsula Walk and eventually, The Loop Track.

"It's too far for you to be walking in the winter." Rob said when she told him. "What if you slipped on the track? It wouldn't take much to break that bone again." She raised her eyes to the heavens, saying a silent prayer for patience, then advised him she'd been taking the walking sticks. Still, this wasn't enough to satisfy him.

She desperately wanted to do the Lake Head walk, but the journey would be a six-hour return tramp.

One chilly afternoon, she broached the subject with Rob. "I'd like to walk up to Lake Head," she said, knowing he wouldn't be happy.

"What do you want to do that for?"

"The exercise."

"There's a walker there," he said, raising a hand and pointing to the elliptical trainer that sat idly in the corner of the room, his eyes still focused on the newspaper. "Use that. I bought it for you."

She turned to look at the exercise machine "And I do use it." She took a deep breath and rushed on. "But I need to be outside. I want to breathe the clean mountain air while I exercise."

"You're not bloody Heidi."

"I know." Rena ducked her head at the stinging comment. Heat rushed to her cheeks. Why didn't he like her going outside? Why couldn't he understand that she liked the outdoors as much, or maybe more than him.

He snorted. "Look, it's a bit far, don't you think? How about you leave it for a while, and then I can come with you."

"Don't you trust me?" Rena asked.

"What do you mean by that?" Icy shards glistened in his eyes. A shiver shot down her spine. "Of course, I trust you. Why wouldn't I? I just think a six-hour walk is a bit far. At least, if I'm with you, I can make you come back if your leg starts to trouble you."

"That's okay. I'll drop it." Tears threatened to fall. She scrubbed at her eyes to make them go away.

Rob rolled his eyes and huffed out a sigh. "Don't be like that, babe. How about we do it this weekend?" His imploring tone didn't sound genuine; more as if he hoped she would turn him down.

"That sounds like a plan," she said, turning to him and smiling brightly. "Saturday would be good."

-o0o-

Rob arrived home late on Friday night.

"Sorry babe," he said, throwing his jacket over the back of a chair, "busy at work. Absolutely whacked. What's for tea?"

"Steak, with chips and salad."

"Salad? At this time of year?" He heaved a sigh. "Guess it's better than nothing." He plonked down at the table and waited for her to serve him. She put the plate in front of him but, before she took her hand away, he grabbed her wrist. "Can't go walking tomorrow, got more work. Gotta make the most of the nice weather."

Rena nodded.

Deep down inside, she had known he'd come up with some excuse.

-oOo-

The next morning, she dressed in warm clothes, shoved her feet into her walking boots and grabbed the rucksack she'd found at the back of the cupboard. She'd already packed the bag with a water bottle, a couple of muesli bars and some chocolate bites. A nice filled roll and some fruit would fill her up for the walk.

"Where are you going?" The mumble came from under the rumpled bed sheets.

"I'm heading off to Lake Head for a walk."

Rob threw the blankets off and turned to glare at her. "The hell you are!"

"Just because you can't go, doesn't mean that I can't."

"You aren't going anywhere."

She stopped lacing up her boots and glared back at him.

"I will go for a walk if I want to."

"No, you won't." He leapt from the bed and grabbed her arms, digging his fingers in painfully. Pinning them to her sides, he pushed her back onto the bed and straddled her. His cold eyes bored into hers.

"When I say you aren't going anywhere, I expect your compliance. Do you understand me?" Spittle escaped his clenched teeth and fell on her face. She blinked. Anger radiated from his tense muscles and, for the first time, she felt scared of him.

"Yes," she squeaked, trying to draw breath into her burning lungs. His weight, pressing on her chest, made it difficult to breathe.

He bent lower until his face was centimetres above hers. "Yes, what?"

"Yes, I understand," she said, a little louder.

His morning breath huffed onto her face as his gaze searched hers, looking for her compliance. Seemingly satisfied, he smiled coldly, eased up a little and let go of her hands. "Good. Pleased you do." He glared and rolled off, keeping his eyes on her.

She sat up slowly, rubbing her arms to return the warmth where he had gripped them. She fumbled undoing her shoelaces under his tight scrutiny and cold stare.

Rob's demeanour, his tone, his stature all screamed bully at her. She glanced at the open doorway, and then her shoulders slumped. Why hadn't she gone with her instincts? Her gut feeling had warned her what he was. Now, she was trapped. She kicked her boots off.

He nodded. "I have work to do," he said, pulling on his uniform. His eyes never left watching her.

He finished dressing and indicated she was to head down to the kitchen before him. Her mouth dried. Stomach clenched, avoiding eye contact, she eased past him. He followed her down the stairs. She half expected him to push or kick her, making her tumble down the stairway. That it didn't happen brought a sigh of relief.

"Make my breakfast," he said. Not a request, an order. He grabbed the key off the hook and went out through the back door. Rena pulled a pan from the cupboard. The door rattled and a muffled clunk sounded through the thick wood. A sharp pain pierced her heart. He'd locked the back door. Cold dread crawled up her spine and settled at the base of her skull. She felt sick.

He intended to make her a prisoner in his home.

She glanced at the front door. Unlike the old-fashioned lock on the back door a deadlock kept it bolted, but a key was still needed to get out.

The windows had screens over them to keep out insects, particularly sand-flies, during the summer months. She'd need a screwdriver to remove them.

Rena's heart sat like a cold lump in her chest. She broke the eggs into the pan and took the bacon out of the refrigerator. Panic was clawing at her throat, making it hard to breathe. She took several deep breaths. The front door burst open, and Rob walked in carrying an armful of logs, which he threw into the basket by the fire. She didn't turn and look at him, instead, she concentrated on the frying pan with the sizzling bacon and eggs.

"That should keep you going for the day." His voice sounded bright and cheerful, as if the physical assault earlier hadn't taken place. She hated the way he could dismiss his actions like that.

"Thank you," she muttered, trying to keep her voice calm, and glanced at him to see if he'd noticed the slight tremble. He seemed oblivious. She placed the food neatly on a plate and poured hot water over the coffee in his cup. After stirring in two sugars, she placed the cup and the plate in front of him at the breakfast bar.

"Not hungry?" he asked through a mouthful of bacon and eggs.

"No." She was lying, but there was no way would food sit in her stomach even if she could eat.

She sat in silence, her head resting on her chin, watching him devour his breakfast. Every mouthful he took made her feel hollow inside.

"What are you doing today?" she asked, desperate for information.

"I'm going trapping. *You'll* stay here and rest that leg of yours." To anyone else, his words would have sounded like concern. She knew better.

And if he locked her in today, the same thing would happen tomorrow, and the day after, and the day after that.

How did I not see what a psychopath he is?

"I'm sure I'll manage. I have a good book."

His eyes narrowed, and he stared at her. but the enthusiasm in her eyes must have looked genuine because he relaxed.

"That's my girl," he said, patting her on the head. He scooped the last mouthful of bacon dripping with egg into his mouth and washed it down with coffee. Then he rose to his feet, picked up both plate and cup and deposited them in the sink before heading up the stairway to the bedroom. A moment later, he was rummaging around in the wardrobe, where he kept his gun safe. She rinsed the dishes and stacked them in the dishwasher, waiting for him to leave.

Finally, he returned to the dining room, two rifles slung over one shoulder and ammunition loaded into a belt along with a gleaming knife. He stood in the doorway and removed the keys from the holder on the wall, all the access keys to the dwelling.

"Have a nice day, babe."

"You too," She forced her lips to curve into a smile and held up her head, so he could kiss her forehead.

"Don't do anything stupid." His icy tone chilled her. He walked out the front door and locked it behind him.

Rena sat down on the chair in the lounge and listened to him load up the car and drive off.

Now, she could sit and cry.

Chapter 5

HALF AN HOUR LATER, when the distinctive diesel rumble of the truck was long gone, Rena headed around the house, trying the bolts on every window. All were locked, the keys removed, except for the louvre window in the toilet.

The size of the small gap didn't deter her.

She grabbed the discarded backpack and checked its contents. She balled up an extra sweatshirt and a blanket and stuffed them into the bag. All the camping gear, including the sleeping bags, was in the garage which would no doubt be locked too, but she didn't have time to look.

Glancing over her shoulder and jumping at every little sound, she raced into the kitchen and grabbed some items from the pantry: Cup-a-Soups, muesli bars, coffee sachets and a packet of chips that she knew she would later regret.

She wouldn't head into town.

That was the first decision she'd made.

Rob would track her down, especially if she went to Sharna's. Rena's gut tightened. Sharna didn't mince words, and Rob couldn't bully her. He had tried, but she simply let his intimidating ways roll over her, without taking any of his crap on board. As a result, Rob avoided the woman as much as possible. But even though Sharna could usually handle him, he was too dangerous right now.

Rena needed to get to safety, and that meant somewhere in the Nelson Lakes Park. She knew the area better than him, and Rob would never think to look for her within his own working territory.

Provided she could make it out of the house, she would head to Lake Rotoroa and down to the highway. Once she'd hitched a ride, disappearing would be easy.

She dressed in warm clothes and strapped her leg to the best of her abilities. The glass slid from the louvre window's slots without difficulty, and she piled them on the tile floor. Then she threw her pack out onto the ground. Easing herself through the tight window frame was a struggle, and she landed awkwardly on the ground, causing pain to ricochet up her sore leg. She rubbed the injury, wincing at the pain, and shifted her weight onto the weakened limb.

Her backpack slung over her shoulders, she limped around to the front of the property. Blood rushed in her ears and each footstep had her heart racing. She expected a hand to clamp down on her shoulder at any moment. The cold prickly feeling made her jittery and she kept checking behind, trying to reassure herself she was safe. She stifled a scream when she nearly tripped over in a hollow in the ground.

The snow lay in uneven patches. If she could avoid walking through them, he would assume she remained inside the dwelling. Another thought froze her to the spot.

Where did he go trapping?

Her knees were weak and unsteady. She needed to get moving and fast.

Half walking, half running, she made her way to the main road that passed through the small village and headed towards the Howard Valley. Every time a car passed, she put out her thumb to hitch a ride. Twice, she dived into the nearby shrubs, thinking the vehicle was Rob's utility. Both were false alarms.

Sometime later, a young couple heading back to the coast picked her up in their family wagon. She sat in the back, clutching her pack close.

"Where are you headed?" the husband, Mike, asked.

"Lake Rotoroa."

"It's pretty there," Trudy, his wife said, turning towards the back seat.

"Yes, I have family there. I'm going to visit them." Rena's voice sounded shrill, and her face flushed with heat. Lying was not something she was comfortable with. She tried to smile, but felt it was more of a grimace. Concern clouded Trudy's eyes before she turned away.

Rena searched through the pack for her mobile phone.

I'M FINE, NEED SPACE, TALK SOON. She sent the text to Sharna. Her friend wouldn't be happy, but she couldn't tell her anything more. If Rob turned up... Better that Sharna didn't know where she was.

"Are you from around here?" Trudy asked.

Rena looked up from her cell phone. "I lived in Nelson for a while. Now I travel around."

"You travel to find work?"

"Yes and no. I freelance my work, but I'm on leave right now. Just catching up with friends."

"Nice." Trudy smiled warmly at her. Rena didn't attempt to smile back. She didn't even want to talk; only want to put some distance between her and Rob.

She rested her head against the headrest. How had things got this bad? Rob had seemed so nice to start with, but then he'd become so angry and controlling. He wasn't happy about her going out and about, and today had been the wake-up call she'd needed.

Her phone beeped.

WHATS UP? ANYTHING I CAN HELP WITH?

Rena's face flushed as she considered her reply. How did she tell Sharna that she had been right, and Rob wasn't who he seemed?

NO. LOVE YOU. XXX

Rena turned off the device and tucked it into the pocket of her bag. She didn't want to talk to Sharna either. Her friend would only give her the "I told you so" speech, like she always did every time Rena tried to talk to her about Rob. Sighing, she shook her head, leant back, and watched the scenery flashing by.

They turned off at Kawatiri Junction and headed south. The further she got from St Arnaud, the more Rena relaxed. She closed her eyes and tried to think of pleasant things, but thoughts of Rob and what had happened that morning echoed around her head. A lump formed in her throat. She'd had such hopes for their relationship.

"Is this the intersection?" Mike said, interrupting her thoughts.

She opened her eyes. "Yes, this is it." Snow was falling, whitening the ground.

"How far up does your family live?" Mike asked.

"At the lake edge. It's all right, I can walk from here."

"Don't be silly. It's snowing, and from the looks of those clouds, it will only get heavier. We'll take you up." He turned up the Lake Rotoroa road.

Rena was stunned by the friendliness of the couple. "Thank you," she muttered, tears stinging her eyes. She sat back as the car snaked up the winding road to the lodge.

The dark clouds had closed in, and snow was falling heavily by the time they arrived at the lake.

"That was lucky then, wasn't it?" Trudy said as the car pulled into the lodge carpark.

Rena opened the door and turned to look at the young loved-up couple. Their clasped hands and friendly banter only deepened the sadness sitting in her chest.

"Thank you so much. I appreciate your kindness."

"Don't worry about it. Need to make sure you're safe," Trudy said. She reached through the window and patted Rena's hand. The gesture was tender. "Do you have much further to go?"

"No, not at all. Thank you, again. Have a safe journey." They both waved as the Mike reversed the car. The lights cut through the gloomy landscape, highlighting the worsening weather.

She'd intended to head up the track to the Sabine hut, but with this weather, that didn't seem like such a good idea. She could freeze before she got there.

She had no money to stay at the lodge. Well, she did, on her bank card, but Rob knew her bank account details. If he checked her account, he'd know where she was.

There was nothing else for it.

She settled the pack across her shoulders and made for the snow-covered track.

Chapter 6

ONCE RENA ENTERED THE forest, less snow lay on the track. But, in places, trees had fallen, and the snow had piled up. Then, she had to wade through drifts of it. The going was mainly easy, but gloomy. Night was fast approaching, and she needed to pick up her pace to reach the hut and safety before darkness obscured all vision. She'd set off at lunchtime but, because of the bone-chilling wind, her leg ached, causing her to walk slower than her normal pace. At four o'clock, she wasn't even halfway there. She'd never reach the hut in time.

Aware of the growing darkness and the soft snowflakes as they fluttered down through the canopy, she tramped the track. She needed to keep moving and stay warm. If she stopped, her body temperature would plummet and hypothermia would set in.

First, her teeth would chatter and moving her extremities would become harder and harder.

She would struggle to walk far, start to hallucinate, and become incoherent. Disorientated, she could wander from the track and become completely lost. Overcome by the need to sleep she would lie down.

Inactivity would lead to death.

Her body might remain undiscovered for days.

Or weeks.

Or years.

She shuddered at the thought. Maybe she should have told Sharna where she was going.

Darkness fell, and although snow highlighted areas of the track, the glimmer was hard to detect at times. She couldn't stop her teeth from chattering, and she pushed herself to move forward, determined to keep warm. But, no matter how hard she tried, she couldn't increase her pace.

She slowed down and ate a muesli bar, the first bite of food she had had during the day. Munching on the tasty snack, she contemplated her next step. She could stop and huddle up under the trees, but the temperature had dropped, probably below zero, and with only her clothing and a blanket for protection from the falling snow, she would freeze to death before morning.

Her cell phone was sitting in the front of her pack. She grabbed it, flicked through the screens, and turned on the light. Now she could see where she was going. At least, where to put her next footfall; the track she was following melted into the darkness. The snow fell in thick flurries, making visibility almost impossible. In these conditions, she could miss the track and become lost.

Then again, her slow pace would make any attempt to reach the hut futile. She wrinkled her brow. There was nothing else for it, she would have to find somewhere she could last the night.

She stumbled on, searching along the fast disappearing track for a likely place to sleep; a hollow or a sheltered spot, like inside a rotting log, but found nothing. Her shoulders slumped. Walking any further was out of the question.

She pulled the blanket out of her bag and slung it over her shoulders. Breath huffing in front of her face, she moved off the track towards a large native tree that had fallen to the earth. Beneath the trunk she found an area big enough to squeeze into and create a burrow of sorts. She removed her bag, wrapped the blanket more tightly around herself, and sat down. Rocking backwards, she manoeuvred her body into the small gap. Curled onto her side and facing outwards, she could watch for anything that moved on the track.

She was racked with weariness, but sleep eluded her. Cold air wafted into her lair, making her teeth clatter, and her hands and feet ached. Fortunately, the woollen beanie pulled down low on her head kept some warmth in her body.

But would it be enough to keep her alive?

A shiver ran down her spine. Soon her entire body was trembling with the cold. Tears sprang to her eyes, but she wiped them away and buried her head in the blanket. The woolly covering stopped the ice-cold air from cooling her lungs too badly.

The betrayal and physical pain Rob had inflicted so casually played through her mind. Her heart ached. If she hadn't run off in an irrational moment of fear, she would be wrapped up warm in her own bed. She squeezed her eyes shut. But then, would things have gotten better? Or become worse?

-o0o-

The sound woke her up. Something large wandered through the bush, crashing heavily through the undergrowth. Her heart raced, but she remained motionless, holding her breath. Cold fingers of fear gripped her body in a tight embrace. She scanned the surroundings for the source of the sound. Many animals like deer and pigs lived in the bush. She hoped it wasn't a hungry pig. The noise ceased, and after a few moments of silence her eyelids slowly lowered, and lowered again, until she slept once more.

-o0o-

He remained frozen on the spot, waiting for her breathing to settle into the quiet wispy huffs that indicated she was once again asleep. The interval wasn't long. He crept closer and looked down upon her sleeping form.

He shook his head. Yes, it was her. He reached out but didn't touch her dark damp hair.

Did she have no common sense? This was the second time he'd found her lying vulnerable in the bush.

How did she manage to get herself into such predicaments?

She shivered in her sleep and her bottom lip trembled. Her face, her body, her spirit mesmerised him. Especially, her spirit. Full of hurt, longing and sadness, it resonated within him.

The reason he'd been drawn to this place was a mystery. Her presence and her distress had tugged at his mind, urging him to come to her aid.

Why her?

The trembles raking her body became more violent. Grumbling to himself, he eased her out from under the rotting log. She tried to resist him, but he ignored her efforts and lifted her up off the cold ground. She wriggled a little and settled in his arms, close against his chest. Warmth radiated into him. Perhaps that was the attraction, her warmth? In return, vital heat from his body entered hers and, slowly, she stopped shivering.

Last time, he had barely touched her. This time, holding her close, he could feel her muscles, tendons, and even her bones connecting to something within himself. The tenuous connection had grown stronger.

He ambled through the tangled foliage to keep the breeze as minimal as possible. She had a thin blanket but it wasn't enough to protect her tiny frame this time.

Only his arms.

-oOo-

Rena woke to the sensation of being moved, carried. She opened her eyes. A pair of strong arms nestled her tightly against an armoured chest. She stiffened and gasped.

"Wh..what? Who...who are you?"

"You don't want to know," the stranger said. His voice was gruff and vaguely familiar.

"Where are you taking me?"

"To the hut."

"Why are you wearing armour?" She nestled herself back into his arms. Her cheek rested against his chest, which was faintly warm, although hard to the touch. She listened to the rhythmic beating of his heart, a slow beat, even the strain of carrying her seemed without effort. He wasn't wheezing or readjusting her. Was he really that strong? Surely, this was only a dream.

Their surroundings were invisible in the pitch black. "How can you see where you're going?"

"Don't worry about that. Rest."

Sleep fogged her brain and she wasn't going to argue with him when she could barely keep her eyes open or her brain functioning. She let his heartbeat lull her back to sleep.

-oOo-

She was flooded in light. Her eyelids fluttered open and she blinked rapidly, her eyes blurring as the brightness hit her retinas.

"Rena? What are you doing here?"

A hand pulled her into the hut. She hesitated, resisting the pull.

"Rena? What's wrong?"

Her vision cleared enough to see the young man's face crumpled in concern. She recognised him as one of Rob's co-workers. "Joseph?" Her mind racing, she stepped into the hut. How did she get here? The last thing she remembered was being carried.

Her brain hurt from thinking and was foggy from sleep and cold. Her teeth chattered, filling her head with unwanted noise. She closed her eyes and stumbled forward, her body feeling disconnected and disjointed.

Chapter 7

RENA SAT SHIVERING ON the seat in front of the fire. Joseph unzipped his sleeping bag and tucked it around her shoulders. She held her hands out towards the flames and rubbed them together. Feeling slowly seeped back into her icy fingertips. Her mind still puzzling over the strange turn of events, she surveyed her surroundings. The large hut contained several bunk beds built into the walls. The fire sat in the centre of the space, allowing the heat to reach all four corners of the room. Several candles, flickering and sputtering every now and again as Joseph hustled past them, cast a dim light across the area.

"How did you get here? What were you doing out there?" Joseph put an arm around her shoulders and rubbed her back. She shifted her gaze to his face. Concern wrinkled his brow and clouded his grey eyes.

"I ... I don't know. I was carried here?" Joseph's face tightened, and he ran a hand through his mousy coloured hair. He didn't believe her. Rena changed the subject.

"As for what I am doing here..." She sighed. "Promise me you won't tell Rob?"

"Promise." The young man leaned closer.

"I wanted to go for a walk and..." She hesitated. Rena didn't want to say what had happened out loud. Rob's behaviour didn't seem real, at least, not now. The incident had happened miles away, days ago it seemed.

"Look, Rob can be ..." Joseph paused for a moment. "... abrupt."

"That's an interesting way of putting it." She smiled weakly. Joseph's soothing tone and quick squeeze of her shoulder confirmed she could confide in him.

"He locked me in the house to stop me going for a tramp when he didn't want me to. I had to escape through a window."

"Rena, I'm sorry."

"Why are you sorry? You didn't do anything wrong."

"I know, but ... well I know what he's like, and I didn't want to interfere."

"Oh, Joseph." Tears welled behind her eyes. They ran down her cheeks, stinging her cold face.

"Come on, Rena, you're safe now."

Rena leaned forward and rested her head on her hands. Sobs echoed off the walls as she let the sorrow go. Joseph continued to rub her back. Slowly, warmth crept back into her body and melted the ice in her bones.

Her teeth finally stopped chattering. Joseph moved away and sounds of bustling came from the kitchen. Moments later, he was holding out a steaming mug of tea, which she accepted with a weak smile.

"I feel so stupid," she said, looking at the young man's kind face. Joseph had always been friendly towards her, but she hadn't seen him around much. No doubt because Rob had kept the handsome young man at arm's length.

"Rena, you didn't know. He comes across as being such a great guy and then... Most of us at work have noticed it too, so it isn't only you."

"Gee, that makes me feel better."

"Sorry, Rena. He always gets possessive of his girlfriends. I would have told you if I'd known how things were, but whenever any of us suggested coming by, he'd put us off. We figured you must be handling things okay. We were wrong. I should've come around and checked in on you."

"He was so caring and helpful when I first met him."

"Yeah, he generally is. So long as he's needed, and you're dependent on him. Look, he's done it before. Don't worry, I won't tell him you're here."

"Thanks, Joseph." She sat back and sipped at the bitter tea. Suddenly, exhausted, she closed her eyes. "What time is it?"

"Eleven. What time did you set out?"

"I was dropped off at the lodge around 12 p.m."

"What possessed you to set off up the track? You know better than that, Rena."

"I know. But if I'd used my card he might have found out. I didn't know where else to go, so I started up the track, figuring I would make it in time. When I knew I wouldn't, I found a sheltered spot under a log, wrapped my blanket around myself and drifted off to sleep. If it weren't for the stranger, I wouldn't have survived the night."

"What stranger?"

"The man who carried me here."

"What man?"

"The man that..." The memory was fuzzy. All she recalled was bright light spilling from the open door and then Joseph looming there looking at her. "He carried me here. I'm sure of it."

"You were standing at the door on your own when I opened it. You looked dazed and confused, but I put that down to hypothermia."

"The first signs had set in, but I warmed up as the stranger carried me."

"Rena, are you sure you weren't hallucinating?"

Rena's eyebrows drew down over her eyes as she shook her head. She was certain she'd been carried most of the way. "Maybe I did walk... I just don't remember."

"Hey, you're safe now, that's all that matters."

"Yeah." She yawned, her eyes tearing up. A sure sign she was tired.

"Here, sleep in my bunk. I'll make up a new bed for myself."

"No, I don't want to put you out."

"You aren't doing that, Rena, please. You need this more than I do. We could snuggle up together."

"No, better we don't." Rena suppressed the shudder that went through her. She didn't feel like that about Joseph, and she didn't want Rob to find out they'd cuddled, even if it was to save her life. He'd most likely rip Joseph to shreds.

"I understand." Joseph's lopsided smile lit his face. He might be a handsome young man, but he was far too young for her.

"Thanks, Joseph."

"I meant what I said. I won't tell him."

"I know."

Joseph helped her rise to her feet and guided her over to the bunks. He settled her inside his sleeping bag, making sure she was snug, before blowing out the nearest candles. She yawned once and blackness overwhelmed her.

Reality merged with fantasy in her head, and she dreamed of tall men with chiselled looks, strong muscular chests, and handsome faces.

Chapter 8

THE NEXT MORNING, RENA woke to a quiet hut. Dappled pale daylight streamed through the windows. She looked around and found the room empty. Sighing, she stretched her muscles. Should she go back to sleep? At least there, she was in control of everything around her. For the first time in a long time, she'd slept well. Her body felt relaxed. The tension normally thrumming through her was gone.

She unzipped the sleeping bag, which held traces of pine and musk, and swung her feet out onto the cold ground. She didn't remember taking her boots off, but she must have. Or had Joseph taken them off? She peeled off the still damp socks, draped them over a chair beside the fire and looked for her pack. Common sense dictated she never went tramping without packing extra pairs. She couldn't see the familiar bag anywhere.

A kettle hanging over the fire puffed out clouds of steam, so she made herself a hot drink using instant coffee from a container she found in the kitchen. She presumed it belonged to Joseph.

He couldn't be too far away.

She stood at the large picture window and surveyed the lake. The water was still, smooth, and reflected the hills and forest around it in fine detail. Snow lay thick on the ground and edged the glassy surface like the border on a printed photograph. Footsteps leading to the lake and back again showed where Joseph had been earlier. Stomping came from outside on the deck. A moment later, Joseph walked in, brushing dampness from his heavy waterproof jacket.

"At least it's stopped snowing," he said, taking off the wet garment and hanging it over a chair. "Did you sleep well?"

"Yes. I don't remember much after I climbed into the sleeping bag."

"No, you wouldn't. You were asleep almost before your head hit the pillow." He smiled. "You certainly snored a lot.

Rena's cheeks heated. "I'm sorry," she said, ducking her head.

Joseph laughed. "I see you found the coffee."

"Yes, thank you."

"No worries." He stared down at her bare feet. "Didn't you bring a pack with you?"

"I had one. I must have forgotten about it when I went to sleep under the log."

"What ... what exactly happened last night? You didn't appear to be making much sense."

"I honestly don't know. I realised I couldn't make it to the hut, and I was tired and cold, so I bunked down under a log. The next thing I recall is someone carrying me. I woke up when you opened the door. I don't remember walking or even sleeping." Rena plonked down on the bench seat. "It's a total blank." She shook her head, trying to dredge up events from the previous evening, but only her dreams came to mind. Reality was outside her grasp. "Perhaps, in a hallucinogenic state, I walked here. That can be the only explanation."

"It's all right. You're safe and that's all that matters."

"But I have so many questions." She blinked back the tears threatening to fall. "Like, where is my pack?" A thought struck her. "Oh no, my cell phone, my wallet. They're all in my bag!"

"Don't worry Rena. You don't need your wallet or phone right now. We'll find your pack."

"Was there any sign of footprints outside?"

"Yeah. One set only, leading to the door. But they were covered with snow, and a slight indent is all that's left of them."

"Did you follow their trail?" she said, her voice tight. The hard chest and strong arms holding her close seemed so real. That sense of comfort couldn't be a dream.

"No, we can do that now if you want?"

All Rena wanted was to sit and do nothing. But finding her pack, especially her phone and wallet, was important. She needed the security of her mobile, even though it wouldn't work here. Besides, if someone else discovered her belongings, Rob might find out and look for her here.

"I'll just put my boots on." She reached for her socks. Warmed by the fire, they made her chilled toes tingle. Pulling on damp boots didn't lessen the brief pleasure of having cosy feet.

The winter sun made the day a pleasant one to be out in the snow. Rena and Joseph tramped down the track in silence, with only the soulful calls of bellbirds and tuis breaking the silence. Joseph's eyebrows slowly rose the further down the track they progressed. They'd travelled quite some distance before the tracks they were following led into the bush. Blanketed in snow, the area looked unfamiliar to Rena.

"I don't...this doesn't look..." she looked around. "I don't remember this—" her voice trailed off. After searching through the undergrowth for a few minutes, Rena found her pack buried under a white mound. Her hands trembled as she clutched it tight to her chest on their way back to the hut.

"You hadn't even made it halfway. How did you walk that far in the dark?" Joseph asked. Rena scratched the back of her neck, frowning as she thought.

"I don't know." Rena shrugged. Separating reality from her dreams was hard. The line was blurred. An image of a strong male body entered her mind, and she shuddered. Instinct told her she had been carried, and carefully. Yet normality said that sounded bizarre.

The sun slid behind the hill, and chill air seeped into her bones again. At least with Joseph beside her, she would reach the hut again in safety.

-o0o-

Darkness fell not long after they arrived back at the hut. Joseph stoked the fire while Rena emptied out her pack and placed its contents out to dry. The muesli bars and fruit went on the bench to share with Joseph. Although she remembered putting it in her pack, she couldn't find her blanket. Vague memories of wrapping herself up in it when she had sheltered under the log teased at her brain. At least she had extra socks and pants. She put the dry clothes on and, after wrapping Joseph's blanket around her, stripped off her two tops and jacket. The tops needed rinsing, so she did that and placed them around the fire to dry as well.

She picked up her phone. The battery had gone flat. Her wallet lay by the fire, steam rising off it.

"The sum total of my entire life at the moment," she said, picking through the remains of rubbish in the bottom of her pack.

Joseph laughed. "Better than nothing."

"There's no books or anything. I usually try and keep a book in my pack."

"You'll find plenty here. People leave books all the time. Have a look."

She hadn't noticed the pile of paperbacks in the corner until he pointed them out. Picking through the pile, she found a tacky romance novel. Not something she normally read; love didn't happen overnight. Love was not lying in wait in any corner of the universe. It didn't happen like that. It hadn't for her. She thought she had feelings for Rob, but after the way he had treated her... She shivered as she remembered him pinning her to the bed and threatening her.

The book was easy reading and the storyline held her interest. A fragrant meaty aroma pulled her back to the present and she looked up. The view through the window had disappeared into complete blackness. A lit candle sat on the table in front of her. No wonder her eyes ached. She blinked rapidly.

Joseph was over at the fire, stirring a pot. Rena hadn't eaten all day and her stomach emitted a loud rumble at the rich smells wafting in the air.

"That smells divine," she said, putting down her book and heading over to the fire.

"It's ready when you are."

Rena ate like she was starving and asked for seconds, savouring every drop of the thick, tasty gravy. "Thanks for that, and sorry I didn't help."

"I left the dishes for you." Joseph laughed when she raised her eyes to the ceiling. "Hey, I'm heading back to St Arnaud and into Nelson tomorrow. I need some more supplies. You'll be all right here?" He gave her no time to reply. "I won't tell anyone that you're here."

"I should be fine." Rena smiled at him, hoping it hid her fast-beating heart.

"The hut's empty at the moment, and I'll be back before anyone's due to arrive. So, help yourself. We have coffee and you have enough food for a couple of days. Are you sure you'll be okay?"

"Yes, I will. Don't worry about me. I like my own company and should be good for a day."

"Okay then. I'll head out first thing in the morning. The snow should have melted by then, and they'll have cleared the roads. Anything you want while I'm in town?"

"No, I should be all right. But when you get back, can I use your vehicle to go to Nelson myself? I promise to bring it back."

"No worries. I'll make sure the gas tank's full for you."

"Thanks. I want to catch up with a couple of friends and make some plans."

"Yeah, I guess you do. A word of caution though. Stay away from Nelson for a while. Try another town until he gets over it, otherwise, he'll stalk you."

"I kind of figured he would." She sighed and rubbed at the ache in her forehead. "I think I'll go and lie down for a bit."

"No worries. Good night. If I don't see you in the morning, I'll only be a couple of days, tops."

Rena's smile was forced. "Don't rush back for my sake."

Joseph nodded and picked up his book, reading by the light of the fire.

Taking her novel, she went to bed, tucking herself into her borrowed sleeping bag and snuggling in. She didn't read much of the book in the pale candlelight before she fell into a deep sleep.

Chapter 9

THE BRIGHTLY SHINING MORNING sun turned the snow on the ground to mush. Rena looked up the path towards the spot from which she'd fallen six months earlier. A small trickle of muddy water ran down the track. Shaking her head, she dismissed the 'if only' and turned away. She had packed her bag with fruit and water, farewelled Joseph as he headed off and then come this way, determined to explore along the edge of the lake.

A thin strip of gravel stood between the water and the shrubs and bush that grew around the lake's rim, making the track less muddy than if she'd travelled through the bush. Occasionally, her foot slipped, and she stepped in the water. But her sturdy boots kept her feet reasonably dry. And, tonight, she would be snug, back in the hut with her footwear drying beside the fire.

Although remaining bright blue above her, the sky darkened over the mountains, becoming cloudier and murkier with each step that took her further around the lake edge. After pushing past some Toetoe grass, she came upon a strange area of land. The land itself wasn't strange, it was the formation of the land. Farther off, through the trees, parallel strips of wood looked as if they were bound together in the form of a fence.

She gazed around and then, curious, walked through the stream to get a closer look. The deeper water poured over the top of her boots, chilling her ankles. She squelched ashore. Closer, she could tell the structure was not a fence but more of a palisade. She reached out and touched the timber covered in lichen and moss. Although Māori had travelled this way, they'd never lived here. So, what was a palisade doing here?

She walked alongside the towering fence until she found an opening.

Bird call seemed the only sign of life. She looked inside, jerking back when a cheeky fantail flitted close to her face. The dead atmosphere within the walls conjured a cold chill that fingered its way down her spine. Ignoring the sense of dread, she stepped through the gap.

The bird song stopped as if the feathered animals had all suddenly been struck dumb. A wafting breeze pushed tendrils of hair off her face. The wind cut through her clothing and ate into her flesh, raising goose bumps. The hairs at the nape of her neck rose. She raised a hand and rubbed at the strange sensation.

Nothing inside the gates indicated anyone lived there, although neither did the area look derelict. The site appeared as if caught in a time-warp. Rena recognised the buildings and the layout. This was a Māori Pa. However, every sign around the place said that no permanent settlements had taken root in the area. Māori had only passed through Marlborough and the Nelson region on their way to the West Coast to get pounamu, or greenstone. They might have stopped and fished for eels and seafood, but never had they built a permanent settlement.

The site was smaller than she would have anticipated, but she recognised the meeting house and the crude square cleared in front of it. The tekoteko and maihi on the front of the meeting house were crudely carved, but their eyes penetrated, as if accusing her of standing on sacred ground. Chills racing along her nerve endings, she stepped with trepidation further inside the pa.

"Hello? Is anybody there?" Her voice echoed around the flat piece of land. She checked all the buildings, including the sleeping huts, but found no signs of recent activity. The gardens, however, were well kept and growing food even though it was the middle of winter.

"Anyone around?" She called again, scanning her surroundings. A dark chasm cutting into the bank that ran up to the hill behind caught her eye. A good place to hide. She approached carefully and stood at the entrance while her eyes slowly adjusted to the darkness within.

"Hello?"

Her voice echoed back at her. She smiled to calm her unsettled nerves and rubbed her hands up her arms. The narrow opening widened into a large chamber. She wished she'd brought a torch with her.

Taking a deep breath, she stepped inside the cave. Water, dripping from the walls, was amplified in the enclosed space. She had no torch, but her eyes adjusted to the dimness, and she edged her way forward. Her pace was slow, but if she tripped and fell, she'd be caught inside the cave without any means of getting out. A large mound appeared in front of her. She raised her foot to clamber over the rock but could find no footing on the tall barrier, so she moved sideways to find her around it. She found a hollow for her foot and heaved herself up. As her leg took her weight, the rock gave way, and she tumbled to the ground. with a cry, her heart racing.

Loud growling filled the cave. "Who dares to enter the cave of the Te Ngakau Pouri?" The voice filled the space with menace.

Rena opened her mouth, but nothing came out. She scrambled to her feet and stumbled backwards towards the light of the entrance. A presence rose before her. She almost tripped as she exited the mouth of the cave. An image emerged from the shadows, his green skin glistening in the sunless atmosphere, his face covered in deeply carved moko. A hei matau, or hook pendant lay prominently amongst the tattoos on his chest. Large spikes, which shifted stiffly as he moved, covered his head. Golden reptilian eyes pierced her, pinning her to the spot.

She opened and closed her mouth, trying to find her voice so she could scream. Her heart hammered so hard inside her chest she waited for it to burst apart. The creature towering over her was menacing, yet his smooth green skin and striking features mesmerised her. He ducked his head to exit the cave, extending himself to his full height, nearly a full metre above her own.

His skin was the same colour as greenstone and flecked with blacks and lighter greens. Defined muscles carved his body, and she let her eyes travel his strong torso down through the navel to his groin. A traditional Māori grass skirt covered that area. Large hands reached towards her. The ends of his elongated fingers ended in claws, and she cowered at the sight.

Something sparked in his eyes. Recognition? The monster lifted his head and howled, the unearthly sound rumbling the ground beneath her. Whatever birds had been around fled in a flurry of feathers. The air around her froze, and her breath huffed misty clouds in front of her face. Her heart rate sped up. Pumping blood pounded in her ears. His gaze returned to her. Cold and vicious eyes raked her body. She took a step backwards.

"It's you," he growled. "You shouldn't have come here."

That voice, she'd heard it before. But where? Her mind raced through possibilities. This angry, mythical creature towering over her spoke English. His voice, deep, earthy, rich... Memory crashed in on her. This ... thing had helped her.

A cold sweat beaded on her forehead. Her voice quavering, she said, "Who are you?"

"I am Te Ngakau Pouri, the Taniwha of Rotoroa. You're trespassing on my property, and now you can never leave." A growl emphasised the last word. The coldness in his eyes chilled her as he advanced. She retreated, one slow step at a time.

She swivelled her eyes from side to side. Where had she entered?

She tripped backwards, landing heavily. "What?" The question came out in a squeak. Her heart jumped into her throat. He was encroaching on her space, bending down towards her. She tried to scuttle backwards, out of his grasp. An icy hand shackled her wrist. She screamed, but no sound came from her mouth. He pulled her towards him. Rena resisted, trying to pull her arm free, but his grip was like iron and just as cold.

And solid, like she was being held by ... a rock!

"You can't leave here. You have come onto sacred ground. You have broken my tapu." He let go of her hand and looked over her shoulder at the open gates. She rubbed her wrist to warm the icy ring circling her skin. and turned her head to follow his gaze.

"Go ahead. Try to leave." A chill shot up her spine, making the hair at the nape of her neck stand on end. What would he do if she turned her back on him? She wrapped her arms around her belly and took another step away from him.

Then, she turned and ran to the entrance. Darkness obscured the view outside the pa.

How had it gotten so dark?

Dismissing the thought, she sprang at the gateway. And crashed into a solid wall. Although the force of the impact didn't hurt, it flung her back to sprawl in the compound.

Te Ngakau Pouri shook his head. He reached a hand down to her and, in a quiet voice, said, "I tried to tell you."

"But I want to go back. I have to go." She rose, dusted herself off and cast a glance at the darkness beyond the gate.

"You can't."

"Why not? You leave. Twice you've left to help me."

"Because I'm part of the land, and the land is part of me. You can't leave unless you're with me." The monster sighed and turned his stormy reptilian eyes on her. "You're stuck here."

"For how long?" Rena's mind was finding his assertion hard to comprehend.

"But ... I must leave; I can't stay here. I promise, I'll not tell anyone you're here, please..." She cringed at her whining tone. "Telling someone is not the issue. You have come onto cursed ground. Now the curse is on you. If only you hadn't come searching for me."

She stared at him. What did he mean?

He snarled, and Rena jumped at the menacing tone. His features suddenly appeared hideous and ugly.

"Surely there's a way for me to leave. I ... I must leave. I have to get back to..." The words shrivelled in her mouth. What did she have to go back to?

Te Ngakau Pouri tilted his head to the side as if waiting for her to finish her sentence.

"What am I going to do?" She plopped onto the ground, and let her pack fall from her shoulders. The taniwha looked at her and shook his head. Rena placed her head in her hands, her mind swirling with possibilities.

Could she make a run for it?

What if she sneaked out when he wasn't looking?

Perhaps he'd woven a spell to keep her there.

How could she believe him?

She looked up. The taniwha had gone. Had she dreamed him? She looked at the gateway and the blackness and mist swirling beyond.

Rena got to her feet and staggered over to the gateway. Tentatively, she reached forward, hesitated for a moment, and then thrust her arm through the invisible barrier.

A strong force pushed against her limb, forcing her to exert more pressure. Soon her muscles ached, and she gave up the futile attempt. She rested her head against the barrier, hoping to see through it or find out exactly what created the obstacle. She closed her eyes and forced her head forward.

The pressure caused an instant headache, but she opened her eyes. A gasp escaped her lips. She could detect movement and motion through the blackness. Wisps of mist in the shape of humans and animals rose and fell around her. Whatever that place was, it scared her. She pulled her head back and inhaled a few deep breaths.

"It's the place of the dead. That is why it forces you back. You can't enter while you still retain a spirit. If you die, your spirit passes into that space." His quiet voice came from behind her. All the menace had gone from his tone, replaced instead by ... resignation. Perhaps he too hoped she would be able to escape.

"Why am I here?" she asked, her voice small.

"I don't know. The spell keeps people away, and they don't see the place."

"I saw the palisades and wondered what it was. That's why I came in."

"How could you see it?" The taniwha's serpentine eyes opened wide and he gasped.

"How should I know?" Rena's tone was shrill.

The taniwha growled, and she shrank back. Then he sighed. "I gave you water from the spring. You drank the water."

"Enchanted water? I must be dreaming." She pinched herself on the arm, and her gouging fingers left an angry red welt.

"This entire area is enchanted. That is why no one else can find it. You see it because you drank water from the spring."

Rena thought back over the two times she had been in the vicinity. "I never drank water from a spring."

"Yes, you did. When you broke your leg. I gave you water from the spring in the cave."

"You did this to me?" Heat rushed into her face, and she clenched her fists. "How the hell could I know not to come here? You never told me who you were. I thought you were some hermit who lived around here. Twice you found me! How did you do that?"

"Because you were distressed. I picked up on that, and I came to help."

"How many people have you *helped* in this way?"

"None."

"Why me?"

"Because..." The taniwha fell silent. His arms dropped to his sides. "You wouldn't understand."

"Try me!" Rena's voice lowered a tone as her anger surged.

"I felt a kindred spirit."

"A kindred spirit? You've trapped me here because of a feeling? You're such a selfish, ungrateful..."

"Who trespassed on my property? I didn't ask you to come here, did I?" His voice boomed across the clearing. "I didn't invite you to come and live with me for eternity. Don't put this all on me."

Rena's anger drained and her face felt cold. "E ... Eternity?"

The taniwha shook his head. Rena let go her breath.

"Eternity for me, not for you. You will grow old and die."

"What?"

"Look, I don't control the curse, and I don't know its limitations. Like me, you'll have to learn to live with it."

"Live with it? I don't want to have to 'live with it'. That's not who I am."

"Neither is it me, but I was also given no choice." Te Ngakau Pouri raised his hands for a moment and then turned and went back to the cave, his shoulders set high.

Rena's scream echoed around the compound and she dropped to her knees. Tears spilled down her cheeks and dripped from her chin onto the hard-packed earth of her prison.

Chapter 10

HE COULDN'T BELIEVE SHE was here.

The *woman* he'd saved *twice*.

How had she found his place?

Why had she tried to find him?

He couldn't be angry with her; he'd doomed her himself when he'd given her water from the spring. But he hadn't expected her to come stumbling into his life because, even though she wouldn't admit it, that is what she'd done.

She had sought *him* out.

And she'd found him. But now, she couldn't leave.

Now she had to share in his curse. He shook his head but didn't feel any sorrow. He couldn't feel anything, any emotion, not with a heart made of pounamu.

She was as drawn to him, as he was to her. But why? What was the connection?

He wanted to comfort the woman, but she wasn't ready for him to do that, and probably never would be. She'd only curse him the same as the chief's son.

He shook his head.

Over the years, he'd raged at the curse placed on him. Then he'd become heavy-hearted and changed his name to Te Ngakau Pouri, distressed of spirit. Now, he was long resigned to his fate.

The curse was unbreakable. How could he make her accept that?

If only she'd stayed away.

A pang of pain pierced his chest, taking his breath.

The *hinemoa* was trying to escape. But her life force would keep her confined within the boundaries of the pa, even when he wasn't there.

Years ago, he'd helped another tramper, but he'd died and entered the spirit world. The pa wasn't far from the gateway at Lake Angelus, where spirits gathered before their journey to Reinga.

Another sharp piercing pain struck him, this time in the head. She was trying to see into the spirit realm. Caught between worlds, the spirits were often with him, but she wouldn't like what she saw there. Fortunately, they didn't venture onto his sacred space. He'd claimed tapu on the land, and the spirits respected it, allowing him his piece of solace. However, once he left his sanctuary, they were free to harass him.

He didn't leave often. Two of the last three occasions had involved the woman who stood ranting and raving in the middle of his pa. He smiled to himself.

He should go out there and settle her down, give her somewhere to stay, but a woman was best left alone when they were waving their hands around and carrying on like she was. He'd learnt that the hard way.

He stood in the cave entrance, hidden by the shadows, and watched her move backwards and forwards while making wild hand gestures. Blonde hair, coming loose from its braid started to fall, framing her oval face.

Her dark blue eyes flashed like chips of ice. That much anger he hadn't seen in generations. She tripped up, and he couldn't help but smile. Something burned within his chest, a discomfort he'd not experienced before. He rubbed at the spot on his sternum, and heat warmed the palm of his hand.

Where had that pain and heat come from?

She hadn't tried to escape; he'd been watching her.

Intense tightness gripped his chest, and he groaned.

He coughed, trying to ease the tension, but it only seemed to constrict him more.

What was happening?

His heart raced, tripping over itself as it beat faster. He gasped, catching his breath, and the pain disappeared as quickly as it had come. Te Ngakau inhaled deeply, welcoming the cold air into his lungs. He sucked in several deep drafts before he relaxed.

Never had he experienced such a feeling.

Did it mean the curse was coming to an end?

And what about the wahine?

He didn't even know her name.

He glanced outside. She was sitting on the ground, her shoulders shaking, her head bowed. Her glossy hair fell over her face. Cautiously, he approached her. As he drew closer, sobs, thick and full of heart-breaking sorrow, twisted his insides.

He touched her shoulder and said softly, "I'll protect you."

The woman didn't lift her head. The sobs became louder and more uncontrollable.

What do I do for an inconsolable female?

He sat down beside her, pulling her against his chest, and patted her back with as soft a touch as he could with his large hands. Her hair was inches from his nose. The fragrance of her body odour, the dampness of the air, and the fragrance of some exotic flower drifted off her. Her body seemed so little in his large lap. He had to handle her gently because his own strength could harm her.

Using a long nail, he carefully swept back her hair, so she would look up into his face.

The sight of her damp cheeks and eyes, swollen and red rimmed, tugged at something inside him. She sniffled back a sob.

He looked into the saddest pair of eyes he'd ever seen. Cradling her shaking body, he whispered, "I'll protect you."

The blueness in her eyes was fathomless. Never had he encountered such a colour. She blinked, and the spell she held over him broke. Once more he saw only sadness.

"Come with me, I'll find you a suitable bed."

"I don't want a suitable bed; I want to go home." She hiccupped.

The whining of the ungrateful *wahine* grated on his nerves.

He sighed. "I know. But I don't expect you to sleep in the cave with me. I doubt you would want to be anywhere near me now."

She looked up at him. Her pensive expression said she was weighing his words. "You're right – about not wanting to be in the cave."

He was content with that for now.

-o0o-

Rena hadn't expected this large, monstrous green creature to wrap her up gently in his arms and allow her to cry. He didn't act much like the taniwha of legends she'd read about. They were hate-filled and vengeful towards men.

She'd allowed him to comfort her, his strong, muscled arms embracing her.

His skin, like polished greenstone, was cool and slick under her fingers, and she'd stroked it as she sobbed, the action soothing.

But the area she stroked warmed up under her fingers, so he absorbed and released heat.

He'd let her cry for a long time until slowly her sobs subsided. Then he tilted her head up. For the first time, she looked at his face, fully. Her eyes travelled from the moko imbedded in his stony features to his reptilian eyes. Kindness glowed in their depths. His gaze sought hers, and she realised beneath that menacing exterior he had a soul. She studied his face. He looked like a traditional Maori pounamu carving. His mouth was heart-shaped, but his lips were pronounced. His nose was sharp and angular. If he'd been human, he would have made a handsome man.

Rena was still in his arms when Te Ngakau stood up. She felt weightless.

He set her down on her feet and said, "I have several whare puni you can choose from." He indicated the huts, set down into the ground on her right. She moved towards them, surprised that they all looked warm and inviting inside. The frigid outside air was settling into her limbs now that the taniwha no longer held her. He knelt and invited her to go inside. She crawled through the opening. Several sleeping platforms made of wood lay on the floors, raising the beds from the damp soil. In the middle of the hut stood a small fireplace.

"Where is the chimney?" She asked.

"Chiminey?" he asked, his tongue tripping over the word. "What is a chiminey?"

A giggle bubbled up, and she clamped her teeth to prevent it escaping. "A *chimney* is a hole in the roof that allows the smoke to go out."

"Why do you want a hole in the roof? That would let the weather come in." His tone was serious.

She glanced up. The thatched roof was blackened from the sooty fire. This hut must have been used before.

She checked the wooden planks. No grass or ferns covered them. But with all the snow that had fallen, nothing would be dry.

She turned to look at the taniwha. Grinning, he pointed to a small mound on the end of the cot.

Almost as if he could read her mind.

"I also have something else you can use." He wandered away, and she scrutinised the large, dark space. If she put the fire closer to the door, the smoke would draw out through that. But as for bedding...she eyeballed the pile on the end of the bed. She reached to feel the fabric; soft and warm fur, feathers, and something scratchy she discovered was an old woollen blanket. She shook it out. Her eyes widened when no dust exploded from it. She lay it on the cot and considered the other blankets. The feather one... While soft to the touch, she cringed at the thought of the dead birds that had contributed to the making of it. She unfolded the bundle of fur. Possum pelts had been cleaned, stretched, and sewn together to create a crude blanket of sorts. She rubbed the soft fur against her face, enjoying the instant warmth and comfort the animal skin gave her. Her fingers fondling the fabric, she breathed out and then inhaled. The smell wasn't unpleasant, but it wasn't an odour she could easily get used to. Not musty or damp. Maybe the smell of the preservative used on the hide. She would have to ask the taniwha what he'd used on it.

She couldn't stop her fingers from playing with the fur, so she placed it atop the woollen blanket. With the hides on the floor, it would provide some insulation against the cold.

Moments later, the taniwha's shadow darkened the doorway. Bent almost double, he passed in to her a large, feather cloak. The soft, plush feathers were warm on her hands. Was it his? The mantle was big enough to fit him. Rena lay it on the bed platform. She could wrap it around her as she slept. But would it be warm enough? She lay down on the feathers and sank into the lushness of it. While she hated the idea of a feather cloak, it was luxurious. Warmth crept up her legs and into her body, dispelling the coldness from her bones.

Her eyes felt heavy, and she lay relaxed and warm in her feathery cocoon.

"Sleep well, I'll talk to you later."

"Please, don't leave me," she called. Her heart leapt in her chest. Loneliness was crushing her. She didn't want to be left alone. The feeling of being wrapped in his arms rushed into her mind.

"I need to sleep also."

"Can you sleep in here, with me? Please?" She cringed at her pleading tone. Whinging was not her thing. But this place and the emptiness... At least another breathing being in the room would help her to cope with the situation better, surely.

The taniwha sighed. His eyes glanced towards his cave and back to hers. He squeezed himself into the tight space and settled on the sleeping platform opposite. She lay down again and, encased in feathers, soon relaxed. Dim light filtered through the small opening, and she stared at the surrounding walls, planning ways she might escape. But her eyes soon drifted shut and the darkness claimed her.

Chapter 11

RENA SURFACED FROM SLEEP and lazily stretched without opening her eyes. Her slumber had been deep. Although her back ached slightly, she felt cocooned and warm, and wakefulness wasn't a welcome option. She snuggled back into the sleeping bag, her thoughts on the strange dream she'd had.

Taniwha, ha!

She opened her eyes, and her heart flipped, pulling her awake. She looked up at the smoke-blackened thatched roof and jerked upright.

She wasn't in her own or Joseph's sleeping bag.

Memory rushed in. She was wrapped in the taniwha's cloak.

A tear pricked the back of her eye.

This was her reality now.

She had escaped from one angry man, only to become a prisoner of another. Her fear and sorrow turned to anger and then she'd cried it out yesterday. She remembered the burning sensation she'd experienced earlier as she'd ranted and raved about how unfair life had been.

Her cheeks heated at how childishly she'd acted. She put her hand over her eyes as her thoughts warred inside her head,

What had happened to smart and sophisticated Rena?

I think she got lost when she gave her life over to Rob.

But look where you are now. How do you get out of this?

Can I get out of this?

Do you want to get out of this?

Hell yes, I want to go back to work, escape as far away from here, from Nelson, as I can. I can't take this anymore.

The mound of blankets opposite moved. Rena froze. The taniwha was stirring. She peered through the fading daylight at his enormous bulk.

"How are you feeling?" His gruff voice boomed in the confined space.

She thought for a moment. "Confused." She sighed and scrubbed a hand through her hair. She couldn't really define *how* she felt. The mass of nerves, sensations, and feelings, all centred in her gut, were mixed up and muddled.

She wanted to leave, to go home. *I want to be with him.* The thought took her unawares, and she had to choke back a cry.

But something drew her to him. Nothing she could place a finger on but, in his presence, she felt secure and comforted.

"Darkness will fall shortly, then we can go hunting."

"Hunting?"

"I need to eat, and no doubt you do too."

"But I don't have a torch. I can't see in the dark."

"But I can."

"Can I stay here?"

"Are you sure you want to? I supposed you'd want to get out."

Had he been listening to her thoughts?

"During the daylight, yes, when I can see my way. You go, and I'll stay here."

"You will be safe here. No one will see you."

"Can I light a fire?"

"Yes, I'll set one for you and light it before I go."

"Thank you."

He started to crawl out of the whare when he turned back to her. "I don't know your name."

"Rena," she smiled.

-o0o-

She wrapped the cloak around her shoulders and crawled through the opening. The darkness brought with it an icy coldness. Even within the confines of this spiritual place, winter still held sway. The cloak kept her feeling warm and somehow safe. She lifted the cloak to her nose and breathed in the dampness of the earth, the scent of nature. The smell wasn't unpleasant.

"What is the cloak made of?"

The taniwha was squeezing himself out through the hole. "Moa and kiwi feathers."

She wrinkled her nose and turned her back on him. Reaching up, she grabbed the cloak to remove it, but instead, a cold breeze chilling her back made her draw it even closer. The warmth was too much for her to discard, so she dismissed the thoughts of extinct species from her mind.

The taniwha gathered a pile of wood and set a fire in the small hearth in the middle of the compound, near to her hut. He dragged over a large log and positioned it for her to sit on.

"Are you sure you'll be all right here on your own?"

"Yes." She smiled. "I'll be fine." Her voice didn't contain much conviction and he looked at her for a long moment.

Suddenly, he doubled over, his finely etched face showing pain.

Rena leapt to her feet and reached out a hand. "Are you all right? What's wrong?"

"I need food." His gruff voice was faint. His smile mirrored his pain. She laid her fingers on his forearm. His body was burning. She snatched back her hand. He turned and lumbered off into the darkness. She listened until his harsh breathing was no longer audible.

Tongues of flame flickering and catching on wood danced in the night air. He must have kept it stored somewhere out of the rain and snow for it to burn so well. The fire mesmerised her, and she sat silent and still. The leaping sparks and flames changed from orange to blue and yellow as they found new sources of fuel.

After a while, a chill seeped into her feet, so she tucked the cloak around them. Then boredom set in. She had no books in her pack and nothing to do.

Her mind drifted to Joseph. Would he come looking for her? Only he wouldn't know she was missing until he returned tomorrow.

As for Rob. She'd been gone for two days. He was sure to be out looking for her. The taniwha said he wouldn't find her. But a part of her hoped he would. Another part remained wary, not wanting him to know where she was.

Am I safe here? Or is this just another prison?

She sighed heavily, picked up a stick and scratched at the dirt. Dirt? Why wasn't it mud? She looked around. No snow or slush lay on the ground. Inside the pa, nowhere was wet. Could rain not penetrate the barrier either? The thought of water made her thirsty. The cave had water, but she'd never find it in the dark. She could see no other source in the compound, and she couldn't leave the pa without the taniwha.

Her mouth became drier as she waited. How long would the taniwha be gone?

-oOo-

Another successful night hunting. But then, he was a predator with sharp hunting skills, and he had asked and thanked Tane and Tongaroa for their bounty.

Ambling back towards the compound, Te Ngakau's thoughts turned to Rena. Why had she come here? What had possessed her to seek him out? He shook his head to clear the questions from his mind. Thinking in circles didn't do his head, or his body, any good.

Rena was here now, and that's all that mattered. He needed to make her welcome. What did she eat? He liked eating raw food, but chances were, she wouldn't feel the same way. Foraging around, he found some roots and shoots she might eat. He would cook the meat, even though the smell would make his stomach turn. Once, the taste of succulent roasted meat would have had him salivating, but that was a lifetime ago.

The unexpected pain stabbing his chest and the burning sensation surrounding his heart had surprised him. He'd never experienced such feelings before. They weren't due to hunger pangs as he'd told Rena. He was at a loss to know what had caused them. He'd hurried off, so she wouldn't see his weakness or the pain in his eyes. Concern he could tolerate, but he didn't want her pity.

The pain scared him. After leaving the compound, he'd burst into a full run and thrown himself into the lake. The icy water had taken his breath away and cooled the heat emanating from his chest. The agonising discomfort had settled into a dull ache.

What was going on? Was he dying?

He couldn't leave Rena now.

The bloody curse.

He had lived for over two centuries. So, why now?

While in the water, he dove down to the depths and found a swarm of eels. He grabbed one of the wriggling fry, swallowed the head he bit off and took it back onto land. At least the food wouldn't be thrashing and writhing around when he took it back to the pa.

He also stumbled upon a pig and killed the animal, piercing it through the heart with his long nails. He nicked its throat, letting the pig bleed out. One less thing to turn Rena against his offerings.

The full moon sat highest in the sky, touching the landscape with a silvery light when he returned to the pa. The fire had reduced to glowing embers, and he added a few sticks of wood, stirring the ashes to set them alight. Rena lay curled up asleep next to the smouldering warmth. He stared at her.

Her skin, bleached of all colour, shone milky-white in the pale moonlight, and her hair was highlighted silver, with darker patches underneath. Pitch black eyelashes silhouetted against her pale cheek feathered out as she screwed up her face, the frown disappearing when she relaxed again. Her soft, smooth lips plumped out grey in the dim light. She might be a pakeha, but in the moonlight she looked like a goddess. Her beauty enchanted him. He sighed, suddenly aware of the cool night air and the food in his arms.

He threw the meat to the ground and gently shook her shoulder.

"Rena?"

"Hmmm?"

He looked down on her silver-coated frame. Her face was peaceful and calm. He had the urge to trace a finger around her cheek and chin but restrained himself.

"Rena, I have some food for you."

She opened her eyes. Her pupils appeared black and large in the muted light, and her normally blue eyes took on a strange silvery glow. A hardness crossed her features when her gaze fixed on him, and he regretted the impulse to wake her.

Her eyelids flickered. "I'm thirsty, do you have any water? Please?"

"Yes," he said, shaking his head. He hadn't thought of her thirst. He went into his cave, picked up a gourd and filled the vessel from the spring at the back of the cave. He returned to find her sitting back on the log, poking the wood in the fire with a stick. He handed her the water.

"Thank you." She gulped long drafts from the gourd.

He ducked his head and, ignoring the thickness in his throat, said, "I got you some horopito and kumara. Also, a tuna and poaka puihi." She looked at him blankly.

"Sorry, eel and pig."

She shuddered. "They're dead."

He confirmed their fate, but that didn't remove the look of disgust from her face. "We'll smoke and dry the eel."

"Can we cook the pig?"

Now he shuddered. Meat cooking smelt worse than meat rotting.

"If that is how you want it, yes, you can cook some pig."

"What is horopito?"

"It is a peppery shoot from a fern plant. Very tasty." He handed her one from the clump lying next to the meat on the ground.

"Do I cook it?"

"You can, or you can eat it raw."

Her eyes clouded, but she slowly raised the food to her mouth. His eyes fixated on her lips as she took a bite and chewed the shoot. They were full and in a slight cupid bow. Her lips moved with the motion.

He wanted to taste those lips.

Where had that thought come from?

She's human, she won't want to kiss a monster like me.

He couldn't take his eyes off her.

She chewed faster, and then she opened her mouth and huffed out a breath. "Hmmm, it is peppery." She smiled as she continued to chew.

The fibrous shoot needed chewing thoroughly to break down the stringiness. But at least she seemed to be enjoying it. He placed the kumara in the fire and covered it with embers. Soon, the vegetable would be soft and cooked through.

"I brought more," he said, indicating the small pile beside her. She peeked over at the pig.

"Could I have some meat, please?"

"Most certainly." He turned his back while he removed the skin from the pig, so she couldn't see him doing it. Using his nails, he sliced off a couple of steaks with great care and handed them to her. Then he turned back and devoured most of the pig, bones, and all.

He threw glances at her over his shoulder. Every time he crunched on the bones, she winced. He tried to chew more silently, but bones didn't crack quietly. Instead, he put the pig to one side and focused on gutting the eel. He pierced it with a stake and placed it over the fire, next to the sticks holding the pig steaks. He sat back and watched to check the meat. Juices dripped into the fire with explosive plops of steam. The aroma of roasted meat assaulted his nostrils, and he wrinkled his nose. At least it was only two steaks, not an entire pig. Pig was best cooked in a hangi. Then he wouldn't have to smell it. Next time.

He breathed through his mouth, blocking the smells from entering his nostrils.

Chapter 12

RENA SHIVERED IN THE brisk dawn. She wrapped the smaller cloak around her shoulders and waited, pacing the compound, for the taniwha to get ready. Exactly what he needed to get ready for, she didn't know. Maybe he was only delaying their excursion. This was the first time she would step foot outside the pa since she'd been imprisoned within its spell. Her body trembled and her heart quivered within her chest at the thought. Butterflies battered against her stomach. Scared the food might come up again, she hadn't eaten breakfast. She looked towards his cave and swung the kete in her hands. Te Ngakau had given her the basket and promised to show her how to make one.

He had warned she might see *unpleasant* things once outside, but he hadn't clarified the word. The taniwha appeared in the mouth of the cave and walked towards her. His green reptilian eyes sought hers.

"Are you ready?" he asked.

She nodded and swallowed hard. He held out a hand and she placed hers in his giant palm. He gently wrapped his long fingers around her hand and warmth seeped into her skin. He looked down, smiled encouragingly and then stepped through the gate.

Rena closed her eyes, expecting the force to push her back. When nothing happened, she opened her eyes. Nothing had changed in her absence. The native bush, pushing close to the palisade, obscured any view into the distance. The air was colder though, and the icy breeze cut through her clothing, chilling her bones.

They followed an unfamiliar path; one she'd not seen when she had stumbled across the pa. The trail led away from the lake and then cut back towards it. She looked for signs of the walking track but found none.

After walking for some time, the taniwha stopped. "This is where we first met," he said, pointing ahead. She looked at the uneven surface and the tree she'd rested against. Her drink bottle lay on the ground. She picked it up and hugged it to her chest.

"So, the track is above us?"

"There is no track in this world."

A shiver raced down her spine. "What do you mean *in this world*?"

"Just what I said. You have entered the spirit world. You will only see human forms drifting through the bush. They will look like ghosts to you. But we are the ghosts."

"I'm dead?" A hard lump settled in her stomach, filling her with dread.

"No, not really. But because we exist on the spiritual plane, we appear like that to people of this time."

Rena shook her head. He made no sense.

Am I dead or not?

She stared at the ground. "Can we go please?"

He squeezed her hand. "Are you all right?"

"No, I'm not." Tightness in her chest constricted her speech. He nodded and moved on. She was grateful for his silence. She needed time to think.

A few moments later, he stopped and pointed at a fern. "That one is edible, but some that look like that are not at all palatable."

"How can I tell if it is poisonous or not?"

"Bring it back to me, and I'll tell you."

"Which part can we eat?"

"The frond. This is a pikopiko fern. You can find a few different varieties, but only some are able to be eaten."

She picked a few of the fronds to keep as a reference. They wandered on until they came across a patch of manuka.

"I know you can make a tea out of this," Rena said.

"Yes, and it is useful as an antiseptic. That plant has many uses."

She took some of the foliage.

"Take some of the bark too."

She thrust the items into her kete.

He led her down towards the lake. "I will swim down and catch us some tuna."

"Could you perhaps find a trout?"

"I don't know if any trout live in here, but other native fish do. I will see what I can find."

"Thank you." She smiled at him. He'd been so kind to her. She appreciated his patience with her. He seemed pleased she was willing to help him out. He waded out and sank below the water without causing a ripple.

Rena settled herself on the small beach, her eyes on the ripples. When he disappeared, she'd half-expected that strange force to attack her. A sense of peace, a feeling she'd not had in a long time, settled over her.

The day warmed up, and the breeze died down. Snow lay on the hills in the distance, except in odd patches. Two days of fine weather had melted it from the ground around the lake. Birds sang in the bush. Tui and bellbirds flew overhead, chasing each other through the branches of the beech trees. Piwakawaka flitted around a nearby bush, chittering away to her.

Her thoughts drifted to Te Ngakau fishing for their dinner. The lake was unfathomable. People had fallen off boats and disappeared into its watery depths.

Did Te Ngakau have anything to do with the disappearances?

She hoped not.

Their friendship was still tentative. His anger had frightened her, but anger wouldn't make him kill...would it? She didn't think so.

"Are you all right?"

The husky voice jolted her out of her musings, making her gasp. She turned. Te Ngakau was standing behind her. "You startled me." She smiled and lowered the hand clasping at her chest.

"Sorry. I came up further down and walked back."

She looked up at him. His wet body glistened as if thousands of green gemstones had been set into his skin. The look suited him.

He studied her face.

"What worries you?" His voice was soft. Concerned. Gentle.

"I... Nothing." She took his proffered hand and stood up, swiping at the small stones that clung her hands and ankles. He held her hand for a moment longer than necessary. She looked at their hands, then up at him. He let go and indicated for her to walk alongside him. She glanced sideways to see if he was annoyed. His face had softened somewhat, the lines no longer so harsh and chiselled. The resulting curves made him look more ... human?

"Those people, the ones who drowned in the lake...?" She let the last part trail off.

"No, it wasn't me, but believe me, the eels in this lake—they are big enough to devour a whole man."

She shuddered again. "Gross!" She turned her head at the low rumble beside her. A smile lit up his face and his dark yellow eyes glittered. Was that a spark of life in the depths?

Their eyes caught. Heat flowed up her neck and settled in her cheeks. She ducked her head.

Why had she blushed?

And why did her heart flutter every time he smiled?

"I don't kill people. I protect the lake and the waterways," he said.

"I didn't think you did..." She couldn't finish the sentence. "If you protect the waterways, then how come you eat the fish and eels?"

"I ask Tane, god of the forest, and Tongaroa, god of the waters. They allow me to take what I need."

Rena's mouth shaped an 'O'. Being literally dumped in the middle of Māori folklore was hard to handle, but she accepted it. What was the alternative?

-o0o-

They reached the pa, and Te Ngakau deposited the fish he'd carried slung over his shoulder. Rena hadn't seen it when he'd surprised her on the beach. He descaled, gutted, and filleted the fish. Then he placed the flesh on a clean rock, ready for the seasonings. She was watching him closely, seemingly intrigued by his actions. Her intense study made him feel clumsy; his fingers now fat huhu grubs instead of useable appendages. He slowed his actions as he placed a pile of manuka bark close to the fire. He'd put it on the flames once the fish had been seasoned. He set fern shoots and horopito leaves on one side of the fish. Then he used thin flax strands to tie the fish back together. He picked up a stick and thrust the sharp point into the ground, so it leaned out over the fire. He tied on the fish, and placed the manuka bark on the embers, pulling them over towards the fish. Smoke wafted up around the fish, curling around it, finding entry into the fleshy parts.

He settled back and stared at Rena. She was watching the thick smoke weave patterns around the cooking food. He closed his eyes, her image still visible on his retinas. She haunted his thoughts, and his pain was increasing daily. Were the two connected?

"How did you learn English so well?"

Her question jerked him out of his reverie. He opened one eye and looked over at her, her features hazy through the curling smoke. Her blue eyes shimmered like Lake Angelus on a fine summer's day.

"I have met people in my travels." She sat up, her eyes wide. He chuckled. "I met Kehu, Thomas Brunner and Charles Heaphy when they were exploring for a route through to the west coast. Kehu brought them up this way."

"Kehu?"

"Yes, he was their Māori guide, although unpaid porter was more like. He led them through here, using the Māori trails to the west coast. He knew of my tribe, so we spoke."

"He saw you?"

"No! Definitely not. I visited him at night. I often visited with fellow Māori in the darkness. Many I frightened because they thought I was wairua, but most were willing to talk to me. Often, they were treated as outcasts for leading the white man. And Kehu was a slave."

"To the white men?" Anger darkened the blue in her eyes, like storm clouds encroaching on Lake Angelus.

"No, he was enslaved to a Whakatu tribe. They allowed him to travel with Brunner and Heaphy so they could get rid of him. Brunner offered money to the tribe and they let Kehu go. They didn't realise he would become an important part of history."

"Except I've never heard of him before."

"That's because you haven't studied the history of the area."

Rena dipped her head.

"Kehu told me about the Europeans settling in, and various encounters with other Māori, and later Pakeha helped me to understand the world outside this area. White man came in, settled the land and expected us to adapt to the Pakeha way."

Fear flickered in Rena's eyes.

"Sorry, speaking of the white man makes me emotional. They have taken away the rights and opinions of my ancestors. We didn't own the land, we respected it. We cared for it, and it cared for us. The Pakeha took that from us."

Te Ngakau caught a glimpse of Rena's ashen face before she bowed her head.

His gut twisted.

"Rena, I'm sorry. I didn't mean to upset you." A tendril of hair hid her face and he pushed the curl behind her ear.

She turned and looked him in the eye. Her burning stare said a conflict was raging within her.

"What is it?" He leaned towards her.

She shook her head.

Something was bothering her. He wanted to press further, but if he did, she might withdraw from him. She'd only just started opening up to him, to allow his friendship. He didn't want to alienate her now.

He put a finger beneath her chin and lifted her head up towards him. "I apologise for my words. I keep letting my opinions get in the way."

A tear slipped down her cheek. Using his other hand, he swiped it away. Her skin was warm under his cool fingers. She shuddered. He pulled his hand away, cursing himself. He wanted to connect with her in a more personal way.

"Why the tears?"

"There is so much injustice in the world. The white man did do some nasty things, but Māori haven't helped themselves." As she looked at him, she could almost see his humanity, what he would look like as a man. It was like he was changing, or was she perhaps seeing a version of him that he once was? She shook her head. "I would rather not get into a political debate. I know nothing of Māori ways or culture..."

"You will learn. I live traditionally enough. Though over time I have adapted to the changes around me."

"You've had to. How could you remain secret otherwise? How many of the local iwi know of you? I thought only a hermit lived out here, but you? I've heard no legend of a taniwha at Lake Rotoroa in the Nelson Lakes."

"Do you think they would want everyone to know that a chieftain's son cursed a warrior?"

"But aren't legends based on truth?"

"I don't know. Maybe a legend about me does exist, but only among certain tribes. I imagine the descendants of my tribe probably don't want to acknowledge my existence."

"Do they know about you?"

"I don't know and, to be honest, I don't care."

-oOo-

Scuffing at the entrance to the hut drew her attention. Te Ngakau entered, a steaming gourd clutched in his hands. She shook her head.

She took a deep breath, accepted the gourd, and drank from it. The hot liquid burnt her mouth and she gasped.

"Careful." The taniwha said.

"Were you...human?"

"Yes, Rena, let me explain. I was human before I became cursed." He sighed. "Showing you might be easier. May I?" Rena hesitated and then nodded. He took the gourd from her hands and sat on the bed beside her.

-oOo-

Te Ngakau placed his hands, one on either side of her face, framing it. He longed to kiss her lips. But after her earlier reaction, he resisted the temptation. Instead, he leaned forward and placed his forehead against hers, moving his hands to grasp her shoulders. Their noses and foreheads were pressed together in a traditional hongi.

Instead of releasing her, he held her there, and said, "Open your mind!" His voice was gravelly, tense with emotion. She opened her eyes and stared into his own.

He watched as her eyelids closed, and then she squinted. He resisted the urge to laugh. Instead he closed his own eyes.

"Relax, take a deep breath..."

-oOo-

Images flitted into her mind...flax rustling in the breeze; tui clicking and chirping; the whomp of keruru wings as two birds flew overhead; flashes of light reflecting off the sea.

A waka in the distance; a yell from someone; panic of the tribe. Running, rushing, quiet filled the land. The pa sat empty, a fire still burning in the foot pit, flax kete left unfinished. Everyone fled into the bush.

The chieftain moved everyone further into the bush, pushing them towards the lagoon. They had to be as far as they could from the sea before the others arrived. Te Raupuhara, the formidable chieftain of Ngati Toa tribe.

"He's gone!" his wife cried.

"Who? Who has gone?"

"Our son!" her cries echoed through the valley.

"Hush!" the chieftain said. He turned to his warriors, but before he could say anything, his youngest warrior, Mātātoa approached.

"I'll find him." Before the chieftain could argue, the young man was off, running back towards the pa. He hadn't seen the boy run off, but his gut told him he was heading back to the pa.

His feet moved quietly over the ground, only leaving footprints as he lifted his taiaha and slowed as he approached the pa. He could see smoke rising from the site, more than when they left; so Te Raupahara had arrived and already sacked their protected village. He sneaked around the base of the steep cliffs, listening as he moved. He came around the point and saw the chieftain's son, Hau Tīhāhā sitting in the sand, his hands and feet bound, bawling like a child. As he was only a young lad, the warriors hadn't bothered to leave a guard with him. He would more than likely end up being their meal for the night. Mātātoa sighed. Hau Tīhāhā was an upstart, his own father despaired at him.

Making sure the way was clear, the young warrior approached him.

"Shhh" he whispered as he laid down his taiaha and used his flint to cut the rope binding the boy's feet.

"Come on," he bent down and picked up the taiaha. He would remove the bonds on his arms once they reached safety. He lifted him to his feet,

"Let's go." He turned and went to move down the beach before he realised that Hau Tīhāhā wasn't behind him. He turned back.

"Undo my arms."

"I will, once we have got moving." He said in a harsh whisper. He looked around but couldn't see anyone.

"No, untie me now." The kid didn't keep his voice down.

Exasperated, Mātātoa picked him up, pushed him over his shoulder and ran down the beach, towards the water and around the corner to a cave. He knew it was hidden from the water and the land. The water was cold as they splashed into the cave, and he walked down to the deepest part, the darkest recess. He'd been here before; he knew where every rock was.

He plonked the boy down on the rocks and held a hand over his mouth. Hau Tīhāhā grumbled and struggled against him, and no matter how much he tried to hush the boy, he wouldn't stop.

They sat in the cave, only moving when the tide came in, having to sit in the cold water for nearly ten hours. All the time, the boy wriggled, but not once did the warrior drop his hand from the kid's mouth.

When he finally did, he tried to use his flint to cut the rope from the boy's wrists, but the water and Hau Tīhāhā's fidgeting had tightened the rope, and he had been unable to remove it.

They were stuck in the cave for two days before they were able to move. All the while they heard Te Raupahara's men hunting for anyone that might have been left behind. Disappointed, they loaded up their canoe with their plunder and headed out to sea.

Once Mātātoa was sure that they were safe, he carried Hau Tīhāhā out of the cave. He ventured up to the fortified pa and looked at the remains. It had been sacked, nothing of value was left. He turned and walked straight into Hau Tīhāhā.

"I was defending our pa." He said defiantly.

The warrior glared at him. "You stupid boy. If they knew who you were, they would have made your father pay for your return. We have nothing of value for that man. They would have killed you and eaten you."

He left, moving down the hill towards the lagoon and towards the track that the tribe would have taken into the forest. He could hear the clumsy footsteps of the boy behind him. The boy's arms were awkwardly tied behind him, and he relied on the warrior to look after him. They spent a week travelling down the coast until they found the tribe.

His mother had smothered him when she found him. She yelled at the warrior for not untying her son. The chieftain looked at the warrior, more aware of the hindrance his son was.

"I couldn't undo the rope, between the water and his moving, it tightened up on his arms, and he complained every time I tried to cut it."

The chieftain clapped him on the shoulder. The look he gave him was sympathetic. He understood.

The healer was able to remove the rope, with Hau Tīhāhā crying and howling. One hand had started to go black, which wasn't a good sign. The healer worked on it, putting warming poultices on it, but his hand remained withered into his adulthood.

-oOo-

The scene fades into a fog, there is movement nearby. Bush moving in a cold wind; booming from nearby group of Kakapo; piwakawaka flitting above. A clearing. Māori gathered, huddled under cloaks of flax and feathers. They were high up in the hills, snow-capped, the mountains mere metres above them.

They all froze as a moa came crashing out of the bush. It looked around before lumbering off back into the forest. Two men jumped up to chase after the large bird.

The warrior wasn't young anymore. He was several season's older, but he kept sentry, while others worked to set up camp for the night. There was a large amount of traffic at the clearing, people moving in from the south, east and west, and they were greeted cordially. Small groups broke off to trade various things, feathers, flax, pounamu, koura, kaimoana., Hau Tīhāhā glared at him every time he looked towards the sentry. Years on, animosity still raged between the two men. A silly matter that the chief's son couldn't let go of. The matter of the twisted hand, and the fact the warrior hadn't cut his bonds when he had told him to. If he had, he wouldn't have the gnarled limb he had now.

Hau Tīhāhā rushed at the warrior tackling him to the ground.

"What is your problem Mātātoa?"

"I haven't got a problem. I'm just carrying out my duty. Someone has to keep an eye out."

"We are safe here, what makes you think we're in danger?" The other man snarled, flexing his moko, making it move menacingly.

"We are never safe. You should've learnt that lesson." Mātātoa said.

Hau Tīhāhā growled. "You constantly like to remind me of that, don't you?"

"No. I do my job, like your father asked of me."

The other Māori spat at him, before getting up and moving back to his pack of men.

Mātātoa climbed to his feet, brushed the dust from his back and sides and picked up his taiaha. Ever since the incident, Hau Tīhāhā had bullied him.

There were only a handful of warriors with their group, and their wives and children as they headed down to the west coast to trade for some pounamu.

One woman, Kakarauri, turned to him, a look of sympathy on her face. She smiled sadly, but Mātātoa lowered his head, avoiding her eye contact. He couldn't acknowledge her. He didn't want her to get into trouble too. She was Hau Tīhāhā's sister.

Noises rumbled from the bush and a large group of men erupted from the undergrowth, covered in fern fronds and bracken. They held clubs and taiahas raised, and with loud shouts they rushed at the small groups encamped in the clearing.

Mātātoa glanced at the chief's son who glares at him.

"You arranged this, didn't you?" Hau Tīhāhā yelled at him. The women scattered and ran for the bushes, some being chased by the invading warriors.

Mātātoa stood his ground, battling with a tall man with a greenstone mere, battering away at his taiaha. He could hear it splintering but kept fending off the blows. Eventually a space opened, and he was able to hit the man in his midriff. The man collapsed, air exploding out of him. Mātātoa jumped up and thrust his taiaha down, spearing it into the man's chest. The woman who'd smiled at him had tripped, and a larger warrior fell on top of her, trying to pin her to the ground as she struggled against him. Mātātoa called out, ran over, clubbing the man over the head several times as rage filled his body. The man raised his hands but couldn't lift his arms high enough to ward off the blows. The warrior knocked the bleeding, unconscious man from Kakarauri and helped her to her feet. She raised her hand to his cheek; her body quivered as she looked him in the eyes. He could see there the love that she had for him there. She tiptoed up and kissed him, then gasped, pushing him aside as a taiaha whistled past his ear, striking her on the shoulder. He turned around to confront the attacker, shocked to see Hau Tīhāhā. Mātātoa knelt to help the woman to her feet, but the chief's son pushed her back down.

"What did you do that for? She's your sister."

"She was my sister, she's a stranger to me now. As are you."

Mātātoa breathed out, trying to stay calm.

"You need to take your sister and flee to safety. You know what these men will do to you two when they find out that you're the chief's children."

"I'm not a child."

A tug on his shoulder made him turn around. Kakarauri was shaking her head as she looked at him, her eyes imploring him not to push her brother any further. "Please, leave, let him be. It isn't worth it."

"You need protection, if he won't come with me, then you will." He looped his arm around her shoulders, sheltering her from the fighting. He turned to hurry into the bush, but a curse behind him made him turn back.

"I refuse to be treated like this!" Hau Tīhāhā raised his club and swung it at Mātātoa's head. Mātātoa raised his taiaha, defending the blow letting Kakarauri go. She called out to him, but he shoved her, and she scampered off into the bush.

"You can't do this; you have to leave. Please." Mātātoa implored.

"How dare you? I'll not leave." He pummelled Mātātoa with blow after blow, each expertly blocked by the able-bodied Maori.

Frustration and hate reflected in Hau Tīhāhā's eyes and face before they rolled back in his head. His body convulsed then he stood tall, seeming to grow above the rest of the men fighting around them. His eyes focused back on Mātātoa. There was a rumble of distant thunder as the sky darkened above them.

Words spewed out of the chief's son's mouth, a flurry of curses and bitterness that had never been heard before by any man.

The battle around them ceased as they watched the deformed man rise above the ground. Light flowed out from him and directed itself towards Mātātoa. The light penetrated his body. His body quivereds, twisting and writhing with piercing pain as the curses surged into his body.

His arms and legs felt stiff and hard, his bones solidified, causing him to cry out.

His organs grew harder and agony flowed through him.

He screamed and collapsed to his hands and knees.

His skin changed, pinchin, and tightening around his muscular frame.

He distanced himself from Hau Tīhāhā and the battle that was recommencing around them.

-oOo-

She opened her eyes, and her head shot back. Her heart pounded loudly in her ears. This is what had happened to Te Ngakau? She pulled away from him and studied his face. His eyes remained closed.

"I've been a taniwha for so long, I've forgotten what it is to be human."

Rena reached up a hand and cupped his face. Te Ngakau leaned into her palm, his eyes opening. His skin warmed under her touch. The spikes on his head quivered.

"I don't know if I will ever be human again."

Chapter 13

RENA SAT IN THE weak winter sun, trying to warm up, but the cold breeze easily cut through the cloak wrapped around her. While she detested the thought of dead birds adorning her shoulders, the feathers were exceptionally warm. She pulled the cloak tighter around herself as she sat on the small beach, waiting for Te Ngakau to return. He'd slid into the lake and swum away, a small wake breaking before him, before he'd dived into the depths of the lake. She shuddered. The water must be freezing.

She picked up a stone, flicked it into the lake and watched the ripples spread out over the flat surface. Bird song was plentiful this morning. She closed her eyes, enjoying the noises and haunting calls that filled the air.

A distant drone, growing louder, interrupted her peaceful moment. She opened her eyes. Although still distant, a boat was approaching. She put up a hand to shade the sun and peered across the lake. Rob was at the wheel. Joseph was sitting at the back of the boat. He turned his head to reveal a large purple bruise colouring the left side of his face.

Rena gasped. She hurried to gather up her kete and moved to hide herself in the bush. While she knew she was a spirit, she didn't want to be seen.

Her mind raced. Here was a chance to escape, to get away. But with Rob? He had locked her in the house and made her a prisoner. The taniwha had been nothing but kindness. Could the spell be broken by leaving?

Rob, as if hearing her thoughts, swivelled his head and his dark eyes in her direction, scanning the shrubs. He fixed on her hiding place. Cold fingers of fear reached around her scalp. Her brain told her to run, but her legs refused to move. Like a rabbit in the headlights, she stood rooted to the spot, her knees trembling.

He turned the boat towards the beach, his cold stare unwavering, pinning her to the spot. Her jelly legs nearly gave out from under her.

Her heartbeat raced and her mouth went dry as she the boat drew nearer.

Joseph's eyes darted about as if he was looking to find her. His voice drifted across the still lake. "She's not there."

"Shut-the-fuck-up!"

Joseph cowered in the back of the boat.

"Run, Rena! Ru—"

She saw the fist hit Joseph before she heard it, the sound of something solid hitting flesh, and Joseph slumped out of sight.

Rena couldn't prevent her audible gasp. Rob's attention swung back to her position. The boat rushed towards her. The motor cut to idling, Rob ran the bow up onto the beach and jumped onto the pebbly shore. Rena tried to run, but her limbs were rubbery, and not responding. She squealed as she watched Rob huff his way up the slippery stones and into the bush, grabbing her hair.

She screeched in pain. He pulled her backwards onto the beach.

Her scalp was on fire. "How...?" He punched her in the face.

Stars sparkled in her vision, and she dropped to her knees. All sense of direction fled, and her body wouldn't respond to the adrenalin which coursed through her veins.

A growl came low in his throat. He grabbed another clump of her hair, tugged her to her feet and dragged her towards the boat. She wrapped her hands around his fist and pulled at his fingers. Her legs wheeled to gain a footing. His long stride denied her the time to get a good foothold.

"Rob! Please!" Her voice caught in her throat. He stopped, pulled her up by her hair before grabbing her throat. She thrashed about, trying to release the grip he had on her neck.

"Shut up, bitch!" Spittle hit her face. He shook her, making her head swing backwards and forwards violently. A black void edged her vision.

"Please," she mumbled through her restricted airway. The word came out slurred. Tears welled in her eyes.

He slapped her face hard. The pain hit her like a hammer, and she sucked in a breath. Stars confused her vision again. The blackness closed in. She tried to focus on the angry face and black eyes staring into hers.

"That's what you get for leaving me, ungrateful, selfish bitch."

She gasped, trying to drag air down into her lungs, and swallowed.

He towed her into the water. The lake's iciness took her breath away and with his tight grip on her neck, blackness was descending upon her. There was a raising sensation as he pulled her up by her neck.

She glimpsed a surging wave tearing towards the shore. Her attacker dropped her, and she landed face first on the gravel. Lancing pain shot up her nose. She winced and inhaled sharply. A mouthful of water rushed into her lungs. The boat's hull scraped along the pebbles next to her.

Hands grabbed her shoulders and pulled her to her feet. She stood, dazed, her mind blank. The boat puttered backwards and drifted out into the deeper part of the lake.

Arms encircled and held her tightly to an armoured chest.

"He can't see you," a gruff voice whispered into her ear. The boat drifted further out.

Suddenly, a figure appeared, standing in the boat, looking towards the shore. Rob, his expression twisted and ugly, had a dark bruise discolouring one side of his face. His gaze raked her body.

Te Ngakau released her from his grasp. She stumbled and almost fell. He wrung out as much water as he could from the feather cloak. It had fallen off her shoulders when Rob had grabbed her. He wrapped the damp cloak around her and held her tight against his body, keeping her upright. The coldness filling her from the inside out eased a little.

"When I get hold of you, I'll kill you. How dare you leave me." Rob turned towards Joseph, who was still slumped in the back of the boat. "If you hadn't hidden her, she would still be in that hut."

"I told you, she wasn't with me."

"That's not what the other ranger told me. You were staying in that hut. And her pack was there. How did her pack get there if she didn't bring it?"

Joseph cringed. Rena was relieved he'd kept her secret, but her insides twisted as she saw what those lies had cost Joseph. He didn't deserve that.

"I can deal with him if you want me too?" The Taniwha said. Suddenly, she was aware of the closeness of him. His torso was pressed up against her back, and his arms were wrapped around her shoulders. Her nerve endings tingled.

"No."

"He doesn't deserve to live."

She turned and smiled at her rescuer, but the smile was fake. She didn't feel any happiness inside, only a numbness. "Have you got what you need?"

"Yes."

"Can we go now?" She asked.

"Are you sure?"

She looked back at Rob and Joseph. The boat was motoring into the middle of the lake, heading up towards the eastern end.

"Yes, I want to go back."

Te Ngakau stepped away from her, and she sighed, His closeness had comforted her. Now the chill wind passing between them wrapped around her wet clothes, and coldness enveloped her. He grasped her hand and they walked slowly back to the pa.

-oOo-

She'd pulled him against her when she'd heard that human's hateful words, and he'd felt her fear. His heart had fired up and pain had pierced his other organs. For the first time ever, his skin twitched and moved.

Te Ngakau was becoming more convinced the pain was not him dying, but his ability to feel his emotions growing. The human's words had caused him a small amount of pain. Not physical, not for himself, but because of Rena. A good woman like her didn't deserve that tongue lashing. He was a bully. So, what had made her go with the man?

He could only imagine her pain.

She had told him of this man, Rob.

He was an *aparangi*, an evil spirit.

A type he had encountered once before.

They reached the pa, and he insisted she go and get out of her wet clothes.

"I'm fine," she muttered.

"If you continue to be stubborn, you will become chilled. Please, Rena."

She looked up at him, her wet hair plastered to her head, only wisps flying free. She shivered again.

He assisted her to the ground next to the smouldering fire and sat her down. Her teeth chattering, she leant towards the glowing embers. The grey sky overhead threatened rain, or sleet, or snow. A wind was picking up, so he needed to get her dry, and fast. He threw a couple of logs on the fire; then gathered the feather cloak and drew it around her shoulders.

"You need to get out of your wet clothes." He left her there while he went to the whare puni and grabbed another cloak, plus the rough woollen blanket. He came back to find Rena hadn't moved.

"Rena," he said in a soft voice, putting a hand on her shoulder. She started at his touch. He pushed strands of her wet hair behind her ears. She looked up at him, her face blank. He eased the cloak off her shoulders and pulled at the bottom of her jersey. "Lift your arms."

"Why?"

"Lift your arms up, I need to get this off you."

"But it's keeping me warm."

"No, it's not, it's drawing heat from your body."

"But I don't want to take it off."

He wasn't going to win by playing nice.

"Rena, it needs to come off. Now! Take it off, or I will rip it off you." He didn't like his bullying tone – it reminded him of the human's tirade – but as long as it worked.

Rena shrugged, lifted her arms up and let him pull the jersey over her head. The merino top and merino singlet underneath were next. Although it was damp, he left her bra on. Her robot-like movements had him worried, and he didn't want her to retreat too far into that state. He cuddled her up in the feather cloak and threw the woollen blanket over it, cocooning her in warmth. Her teeth still chattered.

"Stand." She clambered to her feet and he removed the trackpants and merino leggings, and her socks. He swathed her bottom half in the other cloak and sat her back down on the ground.

The ground was cold but, with the feathery insulation, her cheeks had reddened, and she appeared to be warming up.

"I'm sorry for my sharpness, Rena." His fingers twitched, wanting to touch her, to reassure her, but she stiffened as he spoke. "You needed to get out of those cold, wet clothes," he said, balling up the wet wool. He stood, looking at her for a moment. She didn't speak, so he turned to walk away.

"What will you do with my clothes?" He turned and relaxed a little when her eyes sought his.

"I will hang them up, so they can dry out."

She nodded and closed her eyes.

He hung the wet clothes on a flax rope strung beneath the storehouse, safe from the rain, and returned to the fire. He would cook the eel. They could eat the flesh and then, if he put the rest into a broth, Rena could drink the nourishing soup for the next few days.

Provided she got better.

He was concerned for her. She'd been choked and doused in cold water. Now she was sulking. Was she all right? He was preparing the fish when she shuffled over to the fire. He looked up. Her skin was grey, and her lips were blue. His stomach clenched. Something wasn't right.

"Rena?" He settled her beside the fire. Her body trembled and shook even though she was enfolded in one woollen blanket and two feather cloaks. Her fingernails looked purple. He picked up her hands. They felt like ice. Tears dampened her eyelashes, and she sniffled occasionally.

His heart ached as he watched her. He wanted to share things with her, and for her to share things with him. But it would come.

He hadn't experienced that before, not as a taniwha. Cold and unfeeling in his emotions had been his normal state. Now, his heart was melting, and he could sense things he'd been blind to before he met her. If a smile reached her eyes, she was happy. If it didn't, then she was unhappy. He had never noticed that about people.

He glanced up at her. Her lips were blue, and her teeth continued to chatter. He had the fire blazing and was uncomfortably hot, yet she seemed to be deteriorating. Perhaps she was in shock? That man's words had sounded ugly. How dare he talk to a woman like that. If the man had been in Te Ngakau's tribe, he would have been banished for such behaviour.

He shook his head, trying to dislodge the pictures floating through his head. His past and the incident with Rena seemed connected.

Something about the man's countenance, his stance, was familiar. He couldn't put his finger on it, but he knew the man was dangerous. Was Rena running from this man? He didn't blame her, he was horrible and that didn't quite capture the essence of the man.

This...this woman was a conundrum. She'd been cool with him at the beginning, not that he blamed her, becoming trapped by a curse would drive anyone to distraction. But still, she had listened to all his instructions and followed them as best she could. She hadn't called out to the people on the boat because he'd seen her cowering in the bush. The man lying in the bottom of the boat seemed to be no threat. Not like the one who had grabbed Rena, dragged her to the water, and then nearly drowned her. If he hadn't got there in time... Te Ngakau didn't want to think about it. Killing the man would have been a pleasure, but getting Rena out of the water was more important. She hadn't let him kill the man. As a taniwha, he hadn't answered to anyone.

Why now had he chosen to listen to her?

Chapter 14

TE NGAKAU FUSSED AROUND her as she sat shivering and looking at the fire. Her mind was strangely numb. She tried to move her legs, but they refused to obey.

She went over in her mind, what had happened earlier. How had Rob seen her? The taniwha had said they were like spirits, but Rob had touched her, strangled her, hit her. She'd felt each stinging blow he'd dealt to her. Joseph, though, had not seemed to see her.

In slow motion, she watched as Rob leapt from the bow of the boat, stalked up the beach and reached into the bush, grabbing her by her hair. The darkness in his eyes, the spark of evil she'd seen there, made her cry out in terror.

She replayed the incident with Rob over and over in her mind. If only she'd stood up to him, told him to bugger off. Or if she'd run away. But he'd seen her, even while hidden in the bushes. "Rena." The voice interrupted her memories. She gazed around, not fully aware of her surroundings. A green image swam in front of her, a hand grasped her shoulder and something was placed in her hands.

"Eat." The aroma of cooked meat wafted around her. Her stomach roiled, and she tasted bile at the back of her throat.

She pushed the food away.

"Are you all right?" The soft, kind voice broke through her thoughts.

"I'm fine." She glanced up at Te Ngakau sitting opposite and curved her lips into a faint smile. His gaze was penetrating. She curled over when pains racked her stomach. A rumble erupted from the area and she could taste bile at the back of her throat. Sweat bathed her cold face. A lump was lodged in her throat. She brushed a hand against her cheek and snatched it away at the sharp sting that accompanied her touch. The world blurred and tilted. Te Ngakau sat on his side...or was she lying on her side. Her other cheek burned, and pain pulsed just above her ear. A burst of heat followed by a dash of cold had her trembling, and her teeth chattered uncontrollably.

Cold hands helped her into an upright position. "Can you stand?"

"I ... I don't know." She staggered, her head rolling on her shoulders. Strong arms slid around her and lifted her off her feet. Her face rested against his cold chest, finding relief and discomfort at the same time. Her stomach churned, and saliva filled her mouth.

"I want to be sick," she muttered, a moment before she turned her head and emptied the contents of her stomach onto the ground.

Her breathing faltered as she dry-heaved. Te Ngakau held her hair back from her face and gently rubbed her back until she sat back on her haunches. Cradling her in his arms, he bent down, squeezed them both through the hole of the sleeping hut and placed her on the sleeping mat. She curled up into the foetal position on her side. The movement set every muscle aching. Coarse fabric rubbed on her bruised cheek, and her head pounded, as if she suffered a bad hangover.

Although burning up, she shivered violently.

-o0o-

Rena's drawn out groan echoed in the small space.

Te Ngakau was shocked at the quick deterioration in Rena's condition.

Was it influenza? Many of his own people had succumbed to that dreaded disease.

A shiver raced up his spine. Kehu had told him that tribes had been decimated because of the white man's disease.

He searched his memory for a cure. Manuka grews in the nearby scrub. He scraped off manuka bark, stripped manuka leaves and scratched some bark from the kowhai tree. Back at the fire pit, he put the ingredients into an old gourd and placed a rock in the hot embers to heat. He filled the container near to the top with water from the spring in the cave. Clean and pure, the water had kept him alive for two hundred years, so he hoped it would help to heal Rena.

He picked up the hot stone, made sure it was clean and put it into the gourd. The water hissed, and a small amount erupted out of the vessel. He waited until the bubbling stopped. Then he picked up another rock and repeated the process, boiling the water again. He tested the temperature of the water. While the medicine cooled, his thoughts returned to Rena. He stared at the sleeping hut.

The whare was silent.

Too quiet.

The small fluttering, deep in his stomach, made him feel uneasy. He didn't like the feeling. Like the intense pains that consumed him in her presence, he found the sensation frightening.

What was happening to him?

What was happening to her?

He transferred the mixture into a drinking gourd. The remains of the manuka bark, leaves and kowhai bark he bashed with a rock from the fire, breaking the fibres down. Then he wrapped the paste and a heated rock up in a flax kete and took this and the gourd to the sleeping hut. He crawled in through the hole and checked on her.

She tossed restlessly on the bed and sweat beaded her brow.

"Rena," he said softly, so he wouldn't startle her. Her eyes fluttered open. Pupils swam large in the dark enclosed space.

"Who's there?" Her voice squeaked.

"It's Te Ngakau." He reached out and touched her on the forearm. "Here, I have something for you to drink." She tried to push herself upright but fell back onto the bed. He put down the kete and placed an arm behind her shoulders, supporting her neck, and raised her. Halfway to a sitting position, her hands went to her head.

"The world is spinning," she muttered.

"Here, this will help." Te Ngakau handed her the gourd. She held it awkwardly, her eyes unfocussed. He took it from her and, holding the mouthpiece to her lips, tipped up the container until a little liquid trickled into her mouth.

"It won't taste pleasant, but it should help."

She groaned, and then as the liquid passed over her taste buds, half coughed, spilling some of the liquid down her chin. A small trail of the wet liquid travelled down her neck and disappeared under the neckline of her top. She screwed up her face but continued to sip at the drink. The gourd was a third empty when he wrapped her back up in the warm coverings and put the kete under her neck.

She sighed at his gentle touch.

Centuries had passed since he had last felt the touch of a woman, and there were two girls in the village that had made their intentions clear. He was to be married the winter of their return from the west coast, but he had been turned into a taniwha, and fled. He had never tried to find out what happened to the women. He had appreciated both, had taken both, but neither had made him feel like Rena had.

He placed the feather cloak over her and lay on the bed too. His body might be cold to the touch but, like greenstone, once warmed he retained heat for a while. His chest was warm from the fire, and he positioned himself so she could absorb his heat. She sighed again and snuggled in beside him.

Chapter 15

RENA WOKE UP SHIVERING and pulled the blankets over herself. Her back felt hot, but her front was cold.

"Are you okay?" The familiar voice came from behind her.

"I'm cold," she whispered. After a little shuffling of fabric, another blanket fell over her. She snuggled into it and shifted herself around until she faced Te Ngakau.

"Is that better?" he asked.

She nodded. Her breath, deflecting off his body, came back in humid puffs. His arm reached over and up her back and pulled her closer into him. His large arm warmed her back. She closed her eyes but didn't feel sleepy. Her mind mulled over the previous few hours. Removing her clothes and coming in here was a blank, but she did remember the dunk in the icy lake. Te Ngakau must have put her to bed. Something scraped across her neck when she turned her head. She reached up to scratch the irritation and found a tepid kete lying beneath her. He'd thought to keep her warm as well.

"Have you warmed up?" His voice sounded right in her ear, and his hard arm was pillowing her head. How had she not noticed earlier?

"What happened?"

He hesitated and then said, "You became extremely cold, and I had to warm you up. I made tea, and I put a warm rock under your neck."

She considered his words. Hypothermia. The second time in the last few weeks. No wonder she couldn't remember. Her heavy, hot head meant she wasn't well yet.

He laid a cool hand on her forehead. She rested quietly, enjoying the intimacy of his touch. "Rest, I'll make you more tea." He rose and slipped out of the hut.

Rena lay still, looking out through a gap in the curtain he must have put up to keep out the cold. The moody, grey sky reflected her own dark thoughts. She placed an arm over her eyes, trying to push back the threatening tears. The sight of Rob out on the lake had upset her. He'd known where she was hiding, and that was plain frightening. How had he done that?

And the way he'd treated her. Something at the back of her mind had warned her about him. And Joseph had confirmed her suspicions. Still, she hadn't thought he'd be so violent towards her. Her father had been kind and loving, how had she ended up with someone so mean and nasty?

Because he wasn't mean and nasty to start with.

Yeah, but at the hospital, after she'd been discharged into Sharna's care, he'd been moody with her. Surely that would have triggered something within her?

You were too focused on getting out of hospital.

A tear slid down her face and sat on the shell of her ear. She scrubbed at the cooling trail on her face. No use crying.

"You need to go easy on yourself," Te Ngakau said, entering the whare.

She removed her arm, blinking rapidly. "Can you read my thoughts?"

Memories of thoughts she'd had over the last couple of days made her insides squirm.

"No, of course not. But you've been through a lot, and you have a great deal to process. Be kind to yourself until you've healed, little one." He towered over her, his bulk merging with the shadows in the sleeping hut. Steam rose from the gourd he held out to her.

She pulled herself upright, leant back against the wall of the whare and took the proffered drink. The aroma of manuka leaves wafted into the air. Must be the same concoction he'd given her the previous night. She blew across the top of the liquid to cool it. Her chest rattled with each exhalation. She stiffened, holding her breath. If she had pneumonia or pleurisy, she could die without antibiotics.

"The tea should help. Manuka and honey both have antibiotic properties that should help heal any infection you have. And I've added kowhai bark."

"Are you sure you can't read minds?" Rena smiled into the darkness. He laughed, and his soft, genuine chuckle startled her. She'd not heard him laugh before.

"I heard the wheeze in your breath. I assure you; your secrets are safe within your head." The quiet within the whare puni following his words made his insides tighten.

"How do you know so much about medicines?"

A shadow crossed his eyes. "I learnt while in the tribe. The women share the basic skills to keep us healthy."

"Sorry," she muttered. Her question had prompted painful memories for Te Ngakau. Rena blew across the liquid's surface and took a sip. The tea had a little sweetness, but not a lot. Nothing like normal tea, but the brew eased her breathing. She swallowed another mouthful.

"You have nothing to be sorry about. The women of the tribe taught me. All good warriors need some basic knowledge, so they can heal themselves if they get wounded."

"Good point. But a wound and a sickness are two very different things."

"Yes, but we all get ill, so we all know the ingredients our woman-folk put into the drinks."

"I guess you do." Rena drank a little more. "Tell me about the medicines you use?"

"Why bore you with those details now? You will learn them soon enough."

Rena sighed. Her headache was easing, but her sinuses were feeling tight. She inhaled through her nose, but her nostrils were blocked.

"Finish your drink and rest."

Rena tipped the last of the liquid down her throat. "Will you rest with me?" she asked. Rustling sounded in the darkness and a firm; slightly cool body pressed up against her. She turned onto her side, facing away from him, and pushed herself into his curves. His large arm scooped her up and tucked her into himself, holding her in place. His cool body absorbed her heat like a sponge.

The tea took effect and soon she drifted off to sleep.

Chapter 16

TE NGAKAU SAT IN the whare, staring at Rena's burning body. Her face was slick with sweat, and long strands of her hair were stuck to her damp skin. He had lain next to her for some time, but her temperature had climbed further. If he stayed there, retaining her heat, he would only make her hotter.

She tossed and turned, thrashing around on the bed. He'd constantly had to pull the coverings back over her.

Never had he felt so helpless. If only he could take her pain...

He wiped a hand over his face and slipped out of the hut. He needed to get away, but he didn't want to leave her alone. Anything could happen to her. What if she woke up and he wasn't there? Or what if she...

He didn't want to face that possibility. She wouldn't die. Surely?

He filled a gourd with cold spring water from the cave, took it to the whare and left the container beside Rena's bed. She would need it when she woke up because she would be thirsty.

Te Ngakau went back to his cave, seeking sanctuary in its cool depths. His mind raced. He'd changed, physically, mentally, and emotionally. Some changes were surprising, some encouraging. And he was attracted to this woman. The feeling was almost foreign to him. Different than what he had felt for Kakarauri. The blood thrummed within him, something he hadn't felt for years; there was a youthfulness in his step, a warm bubbliness filled his chest, something that had not been around for a very long time. He was transforming because of his affections for this woman, and yet it scared him. He'd been a taniwha for longer than he had been a man. Would he even become a man again? Or would it kill him instead of returning him to human form.

He closed his eyes and listened to the cacophony of sound echoing off the stony walls. A bellbird called in the distance, and he caught the *whoomph whoomph* of wings as a kereru flew near the compound. Fantails chittered and squeaked. His sensitive ears told him exactly where each bird was.

He saw colours as a taniwha, but in very muted hues, like looking through a yellow lens. Greens were much the same shade, the blues were greener, and flickering flames were various shades of yellow and white.

What would it be like to be human again? Would he miss the oversensitivity to sound? Vision? His sense of self?

He had been trapped inside this body, bitter, angry, consumed by the guilt and rage for too long. He sighed. If anything happened to Rena... A piercing pain lanced his chest.

-oOo-

He was parallel to the whare puni when he heard Rena cry out.

"Rena?"

Her skin was wet, and she had pushed the blankets off herself. He touched her on the arm, and her eyes fluttered open. Fever dulled her blue orbs. Her stare wheeled around the room wildly.

"Rena?" Her gaze settled on him, and then her mouth opened, and her eyes widened.

"Rena? What's wrong?"

She tried to push him away, but he wouldn't let her. She was dreaming, reacting to something in her subconscious. He reached for the gourd of water and offered it to her. Rena shook her head, as she started to realise where was she. She tentatively reached forward and took it from him. She avoided touching him, which made his chest heavy. She took deep gulps, her eyes never leaving his face. Fear flickered in the depths of her eyes and in the pinched white skin around her cheekbones. She continued to stare at him.

"Hush," he said soothed "It's only a nightmare. Lie back down and rest. You need to get better. I'll make you more tea."

He backed out of the whare.

-o0o-

He was hyper aware of her body hot against his, and he was loathe to move her. She had been in and out of consciousness for days, waking up, sweating, with fear in her eyes, or shivering and in pain.

He looked down on her and something stirred in his chest. Perhaps he was falling in love. His heart hammered in his chest, something he'd never experienced before, nor would again, but his was body was also weakening. He'd been a strong, ethereal being for centuries. Becoming human meant frailty, weakness and, eventually, death.

Could he live knowing he would die?

The question ran around in his head as Rena slept on. He smiled.

If she can love me as I am, then I can love her as a man.

The idea, while frightening, appealed to him. But how to become human? The pain made his skin crawl. He tried to be strong for her sake, but could he keep up the subterfuge? If he showed weakness at all, would she panic and flee? She was human. Humans fled from what they didn't understand. His heart plummeted.

Rena, lying on her side, tucked into his broad chest, sighed and mumbled a few words. Seconds later she was sleeping once more. His heart melted. How could he not love her? But could she ever love him?

But then what was society like today? He had resisted going near the villages of Rotoroa and St Arnaud, specifically because he didn't want to be seen or discovered.

Not that Rena had been the first to discover him. He had assisted many a lost tramper, or day tripper, but only in the dead of night. Some had ventured into his territory, but unlike Rena, none had been able to detect the pa. It was only their presence he'd felt. Rena was the first one who had sought him out, for surely that is what had made her explore the edge of the lake in the middle of winter.

Slowly, easing himself away, he allowed her to settle into the soft cushion of feathers. He covered her with cloaks, brushed a soft kiss across her shoulder and cheek and left the whare.

The brisk air outside heightened his senses. but they had dulled compared to what they used to be. He sniffed the air. A foreign presence was in the vicinity. He crouched, crept towards the gates, and scanned the surrounding bush. The purr of a motor came from the lake. The frigid water and icy wind, blowing off the snow-covered mountains, usually kept away people during the winter.

He knew instinctively who it was.

Rob.

A growl grew in his chest and he stalked from the pa into the bush by the water's edge. He slipped into the water without a ripple.

His body, until now immune to the freezing temperature, tingled at the chill.

The boat passed above him, and he nudged it with his shoulder. The motor faltered and then stopped. Te Ngakau sank so he was out of sight. A face appeared over the edge of the boat, looking down into the water. Another face appeared; the young man Rena had told him about. She'd said his name was Joseph. His face was contorted, a swollen black eye, and the occasional shudder and pain glazed his eyes. Te Ngakau surged up towards the vessel and hit it forcibly with one shoulder. The boat heaved to one side and a body tumbled into the water. The man thrashed about, legs churning the water. A face appeared at the edge of the boat. Joseph was the one in the water.

Te Ngakau swam up from the depths of the lake. He grabbed the young man by the torso and pulled him under. He swam as fast as he could to the other side of the lake, while the young man thrashed and pulled against him. He strode out of the water, dropped the young man onto the beach and hurried to conceal himself in the surrounding bush. Joseph coughed and spluttered as he rose to his feet.

"Leave here, before he finds you," Te Ngakau said from the safety of the dark foliage.

"Who are you? What are you?"

"Rena is safe. Go, but don't let him see you, or you will suffer more pain."

"Rena? Where is she?"

Te Ngakau growled. Joseph flinched and scuttled backwards.

The taniwha glared at the young man, who cowered back from him, and turned to leave.

"T ... tell her I'm sorry. I didn't get a chance to warn her. Rob was at the hut before I could hide her stuff. He recognised her bag." The young man fell to his knees, shaking and sobbing. "I didn't want to get her into trouble, I promised her I would keep her secret safe."

"She is safe." Te Ngakau's voice had softened. People cared about Rena, not everyone was out to get her. "She's sorry too. Now leave. You'll freeze to death if you stay here. Go!"

Te Ngakau slid back into the water. He headed back to the boat and gave it one more violent bump. Then he swam towards the cove and dry land. Water sluiced from his body, dripping down his legs, as he walked up onto the pebbly beach. He shuddered. Icy tendrils lingered within his body. He looked out at the boat. Rob was running around the vessel, peering over the side. His sigh was heavy. He'd promised Rena he wouldn't harm Rob. But he wanted to rip the man's arms off and feed him to the eels, alive.

Shivering, his teeth chattering, he rushed back to the pa. The icy lake shouldn't affect him like this. He needed warmth to give him energy, but once gained, it was slow to dissipate and kept out the cold. This chill was at his core. He crawled back to the whare, hoping Rena had remained asleep, snug within the feather nest he'd created.

He lifted the feather cloaks and nestled in, positioning his body around hers. She shivered, and her teeth chattered, but soon she was still. He wrapped his arm around her and drifted off to sleep.

Chapter 17

RENA HAD MOMENTS OF lucidity, and weird dreams. She'd wake up sweating or shivering. At times, nightmares would force her awake, and she would be trembling with her heart pounding in her ears. Rob's face mixed with that of Te Ngakau's, and the chieftain's son. The nightmares mostly consisted of her name being called by Te Ngakau's, before changing to Rob. She would cling to the taniwha for security in her dreams, only to discover it was Rob who was crushing her and suffocating her.

She would wake up, drawing breath and staring wide-eyed into the darkness of the whare, and be comforted by Te Ngakau, who lay beside her. He would calm her with a reassuring back rub, or just whisper to her. She found his voice comforting and, as the fever eased, she spent less and less time trapped in nightmares and more time enjoying his close presence.

She couldn't help it. He'd stayed with her, forcing her to drink vile concoctions, which did make her feel better, and sleep easier. His body had become a constant in her more vivid moments. She reached out to touch him, but hesitated. Why did she want to touch him?

Because he had been there for her, he had waited patiently for her to get better. She smiled at the warm feeling that spread within her tummy.

-oOo-

Her cough persisted for several days, tiring her. Te Ngakau stood guard over her night and day. When she moved anywhere, he stood a pace or two behind her, holding a feather cloak in his hands. When she sat, he draped it around her shoulders and tucked her in tight. His presence, while sometimes suffocating, wasn't menacing.

Once she settled in a spot, he would leave to go and do some jobs. As long as she didn't move or make any unnecessary sounds, he gave her the distance she craved, but as soon as a coughing fit came on, he would hustle her back to the whare puni to rest. Then he'd stay with her until she fell asleep.

He fed her up on kereru, fish and manuka tea, which she drank almost hourly. Every day her strength grew, and she sat up for longer and longer periods.

The fire blazed in front of them, the cold wind kept at bay by the burning native timber. Te Ngakau sat on a log and Rena snuggled between his legs.

She liked this version of him: quiet and attentive. This gentle giant was a far cry from the terrifying monster she'd first encountered.

A gasp came from behind her. She turned. He was clutching his stomach.

She jumped to her feet. "Te Ngakau?" Her voice sounded shrill in the silence. She clasped his head in her hands. His face had paled, and he was panting. "What is it? What's wrong?"

"I don't know."

"How long has this pain been going on?" She tried to catch his eye, but his were closed in a squint. A sweat broke out on his forehead.

"Since you arrived here, four weeks ago."

He bent over and fell face first into the dirt. Her heart pounding loudly in her ears, she struggled to turn him over and put him into the recovery position. She threw more logs on the fire and rushed off to find a gourd of water for him. He was stirring when she arrived back. She stroked his cheek, and his eyes fluttered open.

"The pain," he said, wincing.

She eased his head up and put the gourd to his lips. He sipped greedily, pushed it away and sighed. Slowly, he raised himself up onto his elbows and then into a sitting position. He moved his head, shaking his spikes. Rena sat back on her haunches. His colour darkened to an almost translucent green.

"Are you okay?" Rena asked.

Te Ngakau rose to his full height and shook his head again. "I feel … fine." He said.

-oOo-

Later, they sat by the fire, the flames flickering in the late afternoon and throwing out a bone-warming heat. Rena reached out and touched Te Ngakau. His skin was smooth, cool to the touch, but with a softness not there before. She traced the moko on his face, her fingers following the lines etched on his skin. He still felt clammy. His hands, resting on her waist, pulled her close to him and he groaned.

The colour of his skin had changed dramatically. Gone were the flecked dark greens. Now his skin was greeny grey, a colour that didn't look good on anyone. She'd been hoping his dark tan would filter through.

Her heart ached for him. Had he caught her fever? If he had, she had no idea how to treat him. He opened his eyes and smiled at her. She jerked her hand back.

Her grin was awkward. "Sorry."

"Don't stop, that felt nice," he said.

She sat upright, and hesitantly followed the spiral lines on his face with her forefinger. The tattoo covered his cheeks, his forehead, and his chin. Every inch was marked with black lines; the moko of a warrior. Each painstakingly tapped into his skin with a chisel and ink.

"How did they make the dye?"

"Dye?"

"The ink, on your moko?"

"They used the resin and charcoal from certain trees, mixed them with oil and kept the ink in a special container until it was ready to use. The chisel was dipped into it, then tapped onto the skin, carving the face as if it were wood."

Rena winced, but her fingers continued to trace the lines. She raised her eyes to meet his, and he held her stare. She couldn't help it, but something inside of her warmed up and a happy buzz filled her veins.

Her fingers moved down to his chest, where a pounamu pendant hung, seemingly carved from his body. She hadn't noticed it before, but it was in the shape of a hook. Her fingers moved over the smooth stone.

"Hei matau," he said.

"What?" She looked up at him, her eyebrows low over her eyes.

"The shape. A hook, or hei matau symbolises a connection to the water and is meant to give safe travels to the wearer. I wore this when I was human, and it became part of me as a taniwha."

"It looks like it might be falling off." Rena wiggled the pendant. Te Ngakau flinched. She let the carving go and rested her hand against his chest. "Sorry, does that hurt?"

"No, only feels a little strange, like a scab about to come off."

Heat radiated from him and that wasn't normal.

-oOo-

As Rena improved and became stronger each day, Te Ngakau grew visibly weaker. What this meant for them, they didn't know. Rena sat with him beside the fire. He enjoyed her company, shown by his hand touching hers, or around her waist. She would lean on him, resting her head on his shoulder. He felt like a rock and support for her, but he leaned on her, too.

Chapter 18

"RENA," TE NGAKAU CALLED.

She looked from the kete she was weaving, noticing the wintry air was warming up. The clouds overhead still hung dark and grey, but the wind no longer had that icy chill to it. She looked up as Te Ngakau approached. He doubled over, and a low moan came from his throat. She scrambled to her feet and ran to him. One arm under his shoulder, she helped him towards the fire and sat him down.

"The pains are getting worse?"

"Yes." She studied his complexion and laid a hand on his skin. He was boiling hot under her touch, like magma waiting to erupt, and flaming, yellow flecks tainted his green eyes. His arms circled his bowed torso as if he were trying to hold himself together. "We need to talk," he said.

She nodded and waited for him to continue, almost sure she knew what was coming.

"I don't know what is wrong with me."

"You're sick, that's all. You have a fever."

"It's more than that. I fear I'm dying."

"Dying? Don't say that." Rena wagged her finger at him before putting her hands on her hips.

"I'm not getting better, Rena. I'm becoming weaker by the day."

Tears sprang to her eyes. "You're not dying."

"We have to face facts. If I die—"

"You're not dying," she said again through gritted teeth, blinking to stop the tears from falling.

He reached out a hand and cupped her face. "Rena, if I die, the curse will break, and you will be free."

"You don't know that."

"The curse will die with me."

A tear trickled down her cheek. She wiped it away. Te Ngakau pulled her onto his lap and hugged her. His skin was so hot she had to pull away.

"You don't know if the curse will stop working. And if it does, does that mean I'll go back to the land of the living? How will I get out of here? Rob is still out there. How will I get away from him?" All her unspoken fears tumbled out of her

Te Ngakau rubbed her back, his eyes misty. "I don't know. We need to make a plan. We need to get you away from here because, if he comes back, he will find you."

"How does he do that?"

"He wants you and will stop at nothing to get you back. It is the nature of that man."

"How do you know?"

"He reminds me of someone I once knew. Enough with the questions. We'll pack some provisions and head over Mt Misery towards Mt Travers. I'll take you as close to Rotoiti as I can. Then I'll keep that man occupied on Rotoroa. That should keep him out of your way long enough to get to Whakatu."

"Nelson?"

"Yes, whatever it is called now."

"Will you be able to cope? I mean…"

"I will survive as long as I need, to make sure you're safe." He reached up to his neck. The greenstone pendant was hanging by a mere thread. He pulled on the green strand and the amulet came loose. A small droplet of blood beaded the imprint on his flesh. Rena reached up, entranced by the redness against his pale green skin at the base of his throat. Te Ngakau took her hand and placed the hei matau in her palm. "This will protect you during our travels. Keep it with you." Rena folded her fingers around the warm talisman. No longer part of him, the hei matau cooled in her grasp.

Te Ngakau leant forward and kissed her forehead.

"It is the least I can do for you now. It will keep you safe, and you'll always have a reminder of me."

She looked up into his reptilian eyes, her heart breaking. Her breathing hitched as tears thickened in her throat. She flung herself at him, hugging him, tears falling down her cheeks as she sobbed. She sat huddled in Te Ngakau's protective arms for some time sobbing into his chest.

-o0o-

She stopped crying, and Te Ngakau pushed her away from him.

"We need to gather provisions and get organised. We'll leave in the morning."

"So soon?"

"The thaw is coming. I need to ensure you are safe and away from here before anything happens to me."

"Okay, where do we start?"

"We'll need food. If you can collect pikopiko, manuka leaves and any berries left on the mahoe, I'll find us an eel. and We can smoke it to have on our way."

He stumbled to his feet, and then he doubled over.

"You're not going to make it are you?" Rena asked.

He straightened and stared into her eyes. "I will be fine," he said, brushing off her hand. "We need to—"

A gasp shot from his mouth, and his body stiffened. He was staring behind her. She turned to follow his gaze. Rob was standing inside the palisade.

Chapter 19

"HOW THE HELL...?" THE words died on Rena's lips. Rob's mouth curled up and his eyebrows hung low over eyes that glinted like cold steel. He held a gun in his hands. Te Ngakau grabbed her arm and edged her behind him.

She moved to the side, so she could face the bully. "How dare you come here." she growled.

"I came to get what is mine." Rob's vicious tone sent chills racing down her spine. The hairs on her arms stood on end.

"I'm not yours."

"Yes, you bloody are." He stepped towards them.

"You're Hau Tīhāhā." Te Ngakau's assertion pulled Rena's head around. Eyes wide, the taniwha was staring at the intruder, shaking his head.

"No, I am his descendant. I didn't believe the story passed down through our line until I saw you in the water, the day you attacked the boat. I knew it was you, you dirty little bastard."

"How dare you talk to him like that!" Rena moved closer to Te Ngakau and placed her hands on her hips. Her rising anger heated her cheeks.

"I'll talk to him anyway I like. My ancestor defeated him once, I will finish him off."

He raised the shotgun and aimed it at Te Ngakau.

"No! You can't do this!" Rena stepped in front of her protector.

"Step away Rena," Rob's cold tone made her shudder, but she stood her ground.

"I will not."

"Rena, please. I can handle this," Te Ngakau whispered in her ear.

"He won't shoot me," Rena said, keeping her eyes on Rob. She was his prize, the one he'd come to claim, so she had to take that chance.

"Rena, last warning."

She stood her ground, refusing to move.

Te Ngakau pushed at her.

"No!"

Rob sighed and lowered his gun. She let out the breath she'd been holding. The blow came out of nowhere, and she crumpled to one side. Agony exploded in the left side of her face, blanking her vision and bells rang in her ear. She shook her head. Sounds of tussling and punching came from close by.

"Te Ngakau!" She pushed herself up into a seated position. Her head spun. She closed her eyes for a moment until the world stood still. When they opened again, her vision was clear.

Rob sat atop Te Ngakau, punching him with fists that moved in a blur. Her protector was blocking the blows from hitting his face.

"Rob! No!"

He ignored her. She looked for a weapon and her eyes lighted upon a large stick by the fire. With Rob otherwise engaged, she crawled across the compound undetected. She picked up the lengthy branch. On her feet once more, she swung the weapon in her hands. A part of her was loathe to hurt the man, but then the sickening sound of bones breaking and Te Ngakau's groan stiffened her resolve.

She spun the stick hard and fast, striking Rob's head on the left. His eyes rolled, he toppled off the taniwha and lay prone on the ground.

Rena dropped the makeshift weapon and fell to her knees beside Te Ngakau.

She sucked in a breath. Blood covered his pulpy face, and his lip was split and bleeding. Bruises were turning his arms a darker green. His breathing sounded laboured and every time he inhaled, he winced. She laid a gentle hand on his forehead. He groaned deep within his throat.

"Rena," he rasped, his voice husky.

"I'm here," she whispered. A tear trickled down her cheek. "I won't leave you." She laid her forehead on one of his arms. He hissed, and she shot upright again.

"Get water, from the cave." he muttered. His cough was quickly followed by a moan.

She rose to head towards the cave and came face to face with Rob. She gasped and raised her arms to protect herself, but not fast enough. The blow connected and pain blossomed in the same cheek. Blackness closed in around her as she fell to the ground.

-o0o-

Rena woke to sensations of motion and noise filling her head. Nausea rose in her stomach, and her face throbbed with each heartbeat. She groaned, keeping her eyes shut tight. A few seconds went by before reality sunk in. She was on a boat, so Te Ngakau ... he must be dead. A pain pierced her heart and she held in a sob as her mind reacted to the thought.

"Finally awake then, bitch."

She fluttered her eyes open and struggled to sit up. A wave of dizziness brought her hands to her pounding head. The contents of her stomach rose, and she gagged.

Swallowing back the bile, she said, "Where's Te Ngakau?"

"Your boyfriend is dead." Rob's stony stare confirmed the words. He grabbed a handful of hair and pulled her to her feet. She cried out, tears tumbling down her cheeks as she tried to get him to loosen his grip on her hair. But the pain on her scalp was nothing compared to the cold pain that sat in her chest.

"What are you going to do to me?" Her voice came out in a whisper. Tears prickled at the back of her eyes, and she blinked them away. Rob would prey on any weakness.

The wharf came into view, and Rob slowed the boat. He wheeled the vessel to pull in alongside. "Stay there," he said, patting his right-hand pocket, which bulged ominously. Rena gulped.

She sat, waiting, until he'd tied the boat up. Once done, he held out a hand. She refused to take it and clambered out of the boat. On the wharf, Rob put an arm around her waist, holding her tightly against him. She shuddered. His ranger's car was parked not far away. As they drew nearer to the vehicle, he dug into his pocket, pulled out the keys and, using the remote button, unlocked it. He locked the passenger door from the console and indicated that she get in through the driver's door. With a glare, Rena climbed into the car, shuffling over to rest against the door, as far as possible away from him.

"Unlock the door and jump out of the car, and I will have you put in the psychiatric ward."

"You can't do that. There are rules and procedures."

"Yes, and I know them all." His cold smile spiked her blood with ice.

She shut her mind to his taunts. Te Ngakau. Was he dead? A pain speared through her heart and she caught her breath. If only she'd managed to get some of the water from the cave, it might have given Te Ngakau some strength. She prayed to God, Tane, Tangaroa, and any other deity listening, that he was still alive.

Rob drove the car like a maniac. She clenched her fists when he rounded some corners far too fast. Close to St Arnaud he gripped her thigh tight. "Soon we'll be back at home and then you will be safe."

"As long as you're around, I won't be safe." She turned and glared at him, hoping he could read the hatred in her eyes. He could take her life. But if Te Ngakau wasn't alive, she didn't want to live.

"As long as I'm around, you won't get into any more trouble," he said, pinching her thigh.

Clamping her mouth shut prevented the shout of protest. She pulled at the fingers digging into her leg, but he refused to let go. Finally, giving up, she folded her arms across her chest and stared out the window. They'd be there soon. Her heart pounded wildly, and rushing sounded in her ears. A sure sign she wasn't far off a panic attack. Maybe, though, she could use that to her advantage.

They turned off onto State Highway 6 and headed north. In the clutches of a full-blown panic attack, groaning and panting, she grabbed at her heart.

"What's wrong?" Rob's voice sounded muted through the thudding in her ears, but his tone suggested he was alarmed.

"Heart," she muttered, gulping in air like a goldfish out of water. Her breathing had shortened, and the pain in her chest had tightened.

"You can't be having a heart attack?"

"I don't know." Pain was swallowing any sense of reality.

"Shit," Rob muttered and stepped on the accelerator.

Chapter 20

RENA STUMBLED INTO NELSON Hospital, breathless and bent over. Rob had an arm around her guiding her through the doorway. The two nurses behind the counter looked at each other, and then one came around pushing a wheelchair and immediately wheeled her into the Emergency Department.

"She's complaining of chest pains." The conversation taking place around her was meaningless. Pain, intense and crushing, was squeezing the air from her lungs.

The nurses ushered a protesting Rob out of the room and closed the curtain. Now, if she could control and overcome her attack long enough, she could get help.

One of the nurses asked her several questions. But because her voice wasn't co-operating, Rena couldn't answer. The other nurse hooked her up to an ECG machine, wrapped a blood pressure cuff around her upper arm and put a pulse meter on her finger.

More in control now, she said, "Help. I need help."

"Yes, we know dear, it's all right. We have to run some tests."

"No, I need help, from him." she whispered, pointing towards the curtain. The nurses exchanged a glance and looked back at her.

One of the nurses leant down close to her ear and whispered, "Did he give you the black eye?"

Rena nodded.

"We'll ring the police."

"No, don't. He'll only come and get me."

The nurse patted her shoulder. "Do you have a friend you can call?"

"Yes. Please."

The woman reached into her pocket and pulled out her cell phone. "Text her and tell her to meet you at the bottom entrance," she said, handing the mobile to Rena.

Rena didn't hesitate. Plucking her best friend's number from her memory, she sent Sharna a message.

"Thank you," she said, returning the phone.

The other nurse leaned in. "It's not a heart attack, is it?"

"No, a panic attack, but he doesn't know that."

"Okay. This is what we'll do. She paused for a moment. We'll tell him we're taking you up to ICU." A slight hesitation, and then she added, "Is he your husband?"

"No."

The nurse nodded. "We'll tell him that, because he isn't your relation or next of kin, he can't come in and see you. Then, making sure that he doesn't follow us, we'll take you to the downstairs entrance. Your friend can collect you from there."

"Thank you so much, I really appreciate it."

"You don't know how many people we have had to do this for. However, we do have to ring the police and notify them. But we'll do that after you have left."

"Do you have to ring them?"

"Yes, it is standard practice. We'll make sure you're safe first. Okay?"

"I guess. Thanks for your help."

"No worries. Now, I'll put the oxygen mask on you, and tape a needle onto the back of your hand. We'll need to make this look convincing. And I'll come with you."

"What are your names?" Rena asked, her voice choked with tears.

"I'm Nancy, and this is Donna."

"You guys are amazing. I can't thank you enough."

"Don't worry, Donna will take care of the guy. Who is he?"

"He was my boyfriend, until he locked me in his house. I escaped, but then he hunted me down, smacked me across the face, twice, and threatened to kill me if I told anyone. His name is Rob Mason."

"Okay then, we'll get you ready, and then ship you out of here."

Rena lay back on the bed, her heart overflowing with mixed emotions. Thankful to the nurses; fearful of Rob finding out, shame at seeing Sharna, and an overwhelming sense of sadness and loss. She needed Sharna to take her back to Lake Rotoroa. She needed to find Te Ngakau and make sure he was all right. Because if he wasn't ...

-o0o-

Half an hour later, she was ready. Donna squeezed her hand and went out through the curtain.

"Where is she? I want to see her!" She heard Rob and shuddered, closing her eyes.

"She is resting now, and your attitude won't help her stay calm, so settle down or I will get an orderly to remove you." Donna used her nurses' tone. The rest of their conversation was not audible, and Rena breathed out, not realising she had been holding her breath.

An orderly arrived, and he and Nancy wheeled Rena out of the room and around the corner to the elevator.

Moments later the door slid open on the ground floor.

Sharna, eyes wide and brows raised, rushed to her side. "Rena! What's happened? Shit girl, it's been a few weeks!"

The nurse and orderly pushed the bed through the main lobby area into a side room. Nancy removed the tape from the back of Rena's hand. The orderly stared at the unmarked skin. Rena removed the oxygen mask and smiled as best she could at her friend.

"It's a long story, and we need to get on the road as quickly as possible."

"Will you tell me what is going on?"

"Yes." Rena turned to Nancy. "I will be eternally grateful. Thank you."

"Just look after yourself."

"I will." Rena scuttled out of the room holding Sharna hand. They had no time for hugs.

"Rob is upstairs. They're keeping him busy while I escape. We need to head back to Lake Rotoroa."

The late afternoon air outside was cold, and the sun low to the horizon. Her time in the hospital had been longer than she'd thought. Rena shivered at the change in temperature and waited for Sharna to lead them to her car.

"I'm not taking you back to Lake Rotoroa. Are you out of your mind?"

"No, I'm not. I need to make sure Te Ngakau is all right."

"Who the hell is Te Ngakau?"

"Just get in and drive, please. I'll explain on the way."

Rena turned and looked at the hospital entrance. Her heart in her mouth, she expected to see Rob run out through the doors. Once the car, she breathed a sigh. Now she felt safe. Sharna, sitting in the driver's seat, turned towards her. They stared at each other for a second, and then her friend threw her arms around Rena and pulled her close. The warm embrace broke through Rena's wall, and her eyes prickled with tears threatening to spill.

"I was so bloody worried. Don't you ever do that to me again."

"I promise, but can you please start the car?" Her voice trembled, as did her body and pain lay waiting in her chest. She took a deep breath, but the feeling didn't abate.

"Please, Sharna." Her voice broke and hot tears fell into her lap.

Sharna started the car and drove out of the carpark. "What did he do to you?"

"Remember I told you he'd locked me in the house? Well, I went to Sabine hut and met up with Joseph—"

"Joseph? Te Ngakau? What the bloody hell's been going on?"

A nervous titter escaped Rena's lips. Normally, Sharna was the one talking about a multiple number of men, not her.

-oOo-

Sharna turned towards Rena, her mouth hanging open. "A taniwha? Get out of here!"

Rena had filled her in on the last few weeks' events. "Seriously, a real life taniwha."

"You aren't making any sense, Rena."

"That doesn't matter right now. Making sure Te Ngakau is okay, that's my main priority."

They were passing Wakefield. No lights followed behind them, and Rena's shoulders lowered a little.

"So, what happened to Te Ngakau?"

"I don't know. I really don't—I woke up on the boat with Rob, so I don't know." Tears filled her eyes as pain erupted in her chest again.

"Maybe there is a part of him with you." Sharna pointed out. Rena's face went cold, then she flushed. She felt in her pocket and pulled out the greenstone.

A small kernel of hope curled up in her belly. She clutched the stone in her hand, conscious of the heat in the stone, and hoping with all her heart that it meant he was still alive.

They climbed up Spooners Hill and Sharna's eyes kept flicking up to the mirror. Rena froze, her eyes widening. She twisted in her seat to look out the rear window. A car was coming up behind them. She groaned and slumped back towards the front.

"It can only be him."

"It might not be," Sharna said.

Rena's pulse sped up and sweat dampened her hands. Closer now, the vehicle's headlights lit up the inside of their car. On a small section of straight road, the vehicle swerved into the oncoming lane then back behind them again.

Rena huddled down in her seat. "Slow down, and let them pass," she said, putting a hand on Sharna's arm.

Instead, her friend sped up.

"Let them past!" Rena yelled.

Sharna shook her head, and slowed, indicating to the left. The following vehicle drew level with them. A Department of Conservation sign was plastered on the side of the truck. Rena drew in a breath and slipped down in the seat until her knees were in front of her face. The truck pulled sharply over to the left, narrowly missing the front of the car. Sharna screamed and hit the brakes. The other vehicle shot ahead of them and then came to a standstill. Sharna accelerated fast, veered into the incoming lane, and passed the truck. She tossed her phone at Rena.

"Ring the cops. Now!"

Rena scrambled to retrieve the mobile from the passenger footwell and checked the screen. "There's no cell-phone coverage." She groaned. The band around her chest tightened a notch. He was going to catch them. She grabbed hold of the seat to stop her hands from shaking. The truck's lights once again lit up the car's interior.

"Hold on!" Sharna leant forward slightly. The little car sped up, the engine screaming as they flew down the highway. Suddenly, a loud bang came from behind and the vehicle lurched forward.

Sharna shrieked.

Rena twisted around. The truck was right behind them.

"That bastard! How dare he hit my car!"

Rena flicked open the cell phone case and dialled 111. She hit the call button repeatedly, hoping for an opening in cell phone coverage. Finally, the call went through.

As soon as it was picked up, she yelled, "Help, we're being chased.".

"Slow down madam, do you need the police, ambulance or fire?" The operator said in a slow, calm voice.

Crackling came from the speaker and Rena's heart plummeted. "Police. We're going to lose coverage. Rob Mason. Heading on SH6 Kohatu…" The phone crackled again. "Shit! We're near Nelson!" She shouted before the service cut out.

"Damn!" Tears misted her eyes. Rob had won. Her hands tightened around Sharna's phone.

"What do we do?" Sharna's face shone pale in the darkness.

"I'm sorry Sharna. I shouldn't have involved you, but I didn't know what else to do."

"Don't be silly. I would've been pissed with you if you hadn't texted me."

Another thud, and the vehicle surged forward again whipping their heads back.

"We have to stay on the main highway where there's more chance of coming across a police vehicle," Rena said.

Sharna followed the contours of the road up a steep gradient, and the truck fell back. The car had more acceleration up the hills.

Sharna used the advantage and powered around the corners, both girls bracing themselves each time the car threatened to roll.

The headlights of the following vehicle grew dimmer and eventually disappeared. They hadn't gained much of a lead, but hopefully it would be enough.

Finally, they arrived at Kawatiri Junction and the turn off to Lake Rotoiti. Sharna slammed on the brakes, and the car veered to the right. A police car was sitting in the middle of the road. Several others were parked nearby.

An officer approached and tapped on the driver's window.

Sharna glanced at Rena and lowered the glass.

"Exit the vehicle slowly, please." He stepped back.

Rena gripped the dashboard, her knuckles white. Please no, not now. She had to get to Lake Rotoroa.

"Officer, how are you this evening?" Sharna said, undoing her seatbelt. She opened the door.

Rena leaned across. "We're the ones who rang about Rob Mason. He's following us."

"And he rammed my vehicle," Sharna mumbled, pointing to the back of her car.

The officer bent backwards and glanced at the rear. He raised his eyebrows. "Rob Mason. So, you're Rena Collings?"

"No, she is." Sharna pointed at Rena.

"You are safe now. Park your car over—" The sound of a vehicle speeding around the corner interrupted his instruction.

Sharna turned the key, the car fired up and she careered out of the intersection. The truck hurtled towards the police car. Rena threw her hands up to protect her face, waiting for the impact.

Nothing happened. Rena opened her eyes. The truck had stopped inches from the police car. Police surrounded the vehicle and one officer was clutching a taser.

"Rob Mason? Turn your vehicle off, put your hands above your head and exit slowly."

Rena looked up, straight into the eyes of her attacker. He raised a hand and pointed at her, as if no one else existed. Her heart froze.

Chapter 21

"GET OUT OF THE vehicle, Mr Mason!" The policeman's voice was loud and demanding.

Rena couldn't tear her eyes away. Rob's eyes glittered black in the simulated light. She didn't know this man. His stature appeared bigger. He glared at her, his gaze pinning her to the seat.

"Last warning, Mr Mason. Put your hands above your head and get out of the vehicle now, or we will have to shoot you." The officer released the clip on his belt.

Glaring at Rena, Rob opened the door and, with arms raised, slowly got out of the vehicle. Two officers grabbed him, threw him down on the bonnet of the police car and cuffed him.

A female officer approached Rena's side of the car. Her breath puffed wisps of vapour in the chilly night air. "You can get out now."

Rena shook her head. If she got out of the car, somehow, he would get her. The tension between Rena and Rob was palpable. Neither could take their eyes off the other, but Rena knew she had to break the hold he had over her. A hold that had something to do with

Te Ngakau. Being a descendant, could he curse her too? She shuddered.

"Come on, Sharna, we need to get going," she said, shaking her head and closing her eyes to break the spell that Rob appeared to have over her.

"You aren't going anywhere, Ma'am. We need you to provide a statement."

"I have to go. Te Ngakau is dying, and I have to get to him."

"Who is Te Ngakau?" the woman asked, shaking her head, her eyes scrunched up.

"It's a long story. Te Ngakau was attacked by that man." Sharna said, pointing at Rob.

The woman officer looked over to where the police were holding Rob. Sharna started the engine and slammed the car into reverse, crunching the gears. She swung the vehicle in a wide arc and back onto the road, dodging the officers who tried to stop them. Rena urged her on. She still a five-hour tramp. Three, if she could run it.

Inky darkness surrounded them, and the road became slick with ice. Sharna handled the conditions well.

The pre-dawn grey settled around them as they continued to drive. A wave of tiredness swept over Rena. Her eyes felt heavy and her limbs were freezing up. At least, a run in the fresh air would get her body moving and wake her up.

Sharna pulled in at the lakeside. Mist rose off the water, making it look eerie and isolated. No birds sung the morning in. They had more sense than to be out in the cold. Rena sighed and opened the door. Swinging her legs out of the vehicle took a colossal effort. Slowly, she put weight on her feet, but her legs buckled underneath her.

"Rena, you can't do this."

"I have to, Sharna." Rena's vision blurred and her face burned. "I have to find him."

"Can't you have a nap first?"

"No, which part of life or death don't you understand?" She huffed. She looked at Sharna and saw that she'd hurt her friend. "Sorry, I don't have time."

Sharna's gaze was intent. She shook her head. "He bloody well better be worth it," she muttered.

Rena hugged her friend, and Sharna squeezed her back tightly.

Sharna stepped away and slapped her on the back. "You'd better get going then."

Rena grinned, and her body surged with energy. Frost crunched underfoot as she jogged to the start of the track. She turned and waved at Sharna, receiving a half-hearted response in return.

The dark forest interior grew lighter with the dawn, making the track easier to see. She ran as often as she could, forcing down the urge to stop and rest, and instead reducing her speed to a fast walk. Her body ached, her heart ached, her head ached. She hadn't had a bite to eat or anything to drink since yesterday afternoon. That her body still functioned, amazed her. Her intentions focused on Te Ngakau. She had to get to him before it was too late.

Her heart thudded. The thought of him dead... She shied away from that notion. Somehow, Rob had taken her from the pa, but how? Had he broken the curse? Did that mean Te Ngakau was ...?

Her legs pumped faster as she zig-zagged her way along the path. The frozen air chilled her face, and two trails of salty tears stung her cheeks. She stumbled but caught herself before falling on her face. Breathing heavily, she berated herself before pushing on towards the pa.

A faint drone reverberated in the still morning air. The further along the path, the louder the sound. Then she heard shouting. She turned and glanced through the trees towards the lake and caught a glimpse of a small runabout.

"Rena! Jump in!" The voice was Sharna's.

Rena came to a standstill. How had …? A thread of hope wove through her thoughts. Her limbs tingling, she struggled through the bush to the lakeside. Rob's boat was puttering in the shallows. Joseph and Sharna, with a smug smirk and a nod towards Joseph, stood in the boat.

"Come on, we'll get you there faster."

Rena didn't hesitate. She waded through the icy water and launched herself at the side of the vessel. Joseph reached over and dragged her onboard.

"Sharna told me you needed help. But I don't know where to go."

Rena's chattering teeth prevented any speech. She pointed towards the head of the lake. Joseph nodded. Sharna threw a blanket over her shoulders and Rena pulled it tight, grateful for its limited warmth. She set her feet apart and stood tall beside Joseph as he pushed the throttle forward.

The boat lurched ahead, picked up speed and planed across the glassy surface. Ducks and swans, squawking their anger, swam out of the way. The wind cut through the thin blanket and Rena, her eyes fixed on the coastline and eager to spot a familiar landmark, shivered. They whisked past the Sabine hut, and she tapped Joseph on the shoulder. He pulled back the throttle, allowing the boat to slow. Rena needed to get her bearings. She glanced around, looking for the beach and the delta where the pa was situated, but couldn't recognise anything from the lake.

"Put me ashore, please."

Joseph nodded and ran the bow up onto the nearest shingle beach. Rena jumped down onto the pebbles, the blanket still draped around her shoulders. She pushed the boat back out into the water before Sharna or Joseph could follow suit.

"Don't come after me," she said, tears blurring her vision. Whatever happened, she didn't want them trapped in the curse with her.

"He saved my life, Rena, this taniwha of yours." Joseph held her gaze as he spoke. "I hope he's okay."

Rena turned and scanned her surroundings. She headed east, crashing through the scrub. A change in the atmosphere, as if a spiritual barrier had been put in place, told her she was nearly there. Fingers of fear pulled at her resolve. Determined, she pushed through the thick air and found the gate to the pa. The image shimmered. She ran forwards, gasping, and launched herself at the disappearing entranceway.

Chapter 22

SHE LANDED HEAVILY AND tucked her head under to roll into a clumsy forward somersault. She landed next to the whare puni. Staggering to her feet, she glanced around. A large mass lay near the entrance to the cave.

"Te Ngakau!" she screamed, running to drop to her knees on the ground next to the body. She pulled him over onto his back. His sickly green face was clammy to the touch. She wiped a hand across his forehead.

"Te Ngakau?" she whispered.

He stirred, mumbled, and his eyes fluttered but did not open. She picked up one of his hands, holding it to her cheek, cooling her skin.

He smiled. "Rena?"

She laughed, tears streaming down her cheeks. "Yes."

He didn't have long. His face was pale, and the pulse in his hand was erratic, not steady and rhythmic like normal. She checked him over but could detect no external wounds.

She bent forward, her hair spilling over his face, framing it. She leaned down and kissed his forehead.

"Please, Te Ngakau. For me?" She willed him to fight, to live. She couldn't lose him. Not now.

"Come on, fight for me." Her voice cracked.

His breathing became more ragged, and small droplets of blood flecked his mouth. "Wahine, Rena," he mumbled.

Her heart was dying, each beat painful as she watched the love of her life die before her. She sobbed. "I'm here, my love, my aroha.'

He coughed, and his body tensed.

She hugged him close, willing her own lifeforce to keep his going, although she knew it was futile.

"Te Ngakau, I love you. I love you, you silly beast. Now come back to me and tell me you love me too." Her tears fell across his face, A faint smile pulled on his lips. Then one long breath escaped with an ominous hiss. She watched. But he didn't breathe in again.

She turned her head up to the bright blue sky and howled. Her cry resounded ethereal and piercing. A hand touched her shoulder and then pulled her into an embrace. Sharna's eyes too glistened with tears. Rena fell into her arms, her heart shattering into a million pieces.

She had found her only love, Te Ngakau, and now he was dead. How could she live without him? She didn't want to. She wanted to lie down next to him and follow him into the spirit world.

In their brief weeks together, she had learned so much from him, and she didn't want to exist outside of this little oasis of calm and quietness. Her world wouldn't be the same without him.

Someone touched her shoulder, and she looked up. Joseph was standing next to Sharna, one hand on each of them and his eyes on Te Ngakau. Joseph ran his hand over his hair, pain etched on his face. Rena's body heaved with unshed tears. Her breath hitched as she tried to calm down, but her body, her shattered heart wouldn't let her. It didn't want to feel calm or centred. It wanted to let out the pain that had splintered through every cell of her body, through every piece of her existence.

She sat on the ground, staring at his body. Her limbs were numb, her mind was numb and her heart beat cold.

"Come on, Rena, there's nothing you can do for him now." Sharna whispered. She knelt beside Rena and put an arm around her friend's shoulders.

Rena sat like a statue. Even her declaration of love hadn't saved him. How could she live without him?

"Rena?" Joseph spoke quietly. He bent down and grasped her other shoulder. He and Sharna pulled her to her feet. Her unsteady legs buckled. They turned her around, but her eyes stayed on the body of the...taniwha?

No, he was a man.

The *man* she had learned to love.

They exited the pa site and headed towards the beach. The sound of the beating wings of a thousand native birds, closed in around them. A fantail chittered and swung down low in front of them, its tail fanned out like its name. Rena gave a sad smile as she looked at the cheeky bird, one whom she had seen on a regular basis during her stay, but as the bird turned its head, in her heart, she knew that it was saying goodbye. A sob wracked her body and her limbs went limp. Joseph and Sharna caught her weight and stumbled. A bellbird flitted out of the bush, calling out and a tui joined the chorus. Suddenly birds were singing all around them, an unusual thing for winter. They lamented the loss of the taniwha, Te Ngakau Pouri. Joseph, Sharna and Rena stood transfixed on the beach, looking around at the congregating birds, listening to their lament.

Joseph held the boat as she turned towards the site of the pa, now looking dilapidated and forlorn. A cold breeze whipped across the water, chilling Rena to the bone. A mist rose into the air, hesitated, then headed south, towards Lake Angelus, the resting place of the souls. The bird song grew to a crescendo before dying away as they followed the mist into the distance.

Rena collapsed onto the sand, and Joseph helped Sharna lift her into the boat. She allowed them to pull her up, doing little to assist them. How could she? She didn't want to live.

A rumbling from inside the pa site made them all freeze. The cold breeze grew in intensity, chilling them to the bone. Rena raised her head, looking towards the gates. A fantail started to chirp, as if gossiping about what was happening.

Rena leapt over the side and ploughed her way through the icy water. She kept walking, curiosity burning within her. She ran through the gates, and her eyes went to where she'd last seen Te Ngakau. His body was gone. Only thin flakes of greenstone littered the ground.

How could that be possible?

She edged further into the compound.

"Te Ngakau?" Her voice echoed around the empty space. The area seemed devoid of all air and atmosphere. Her breaths came in shallow puffs that clouded around her face. All that existed was the fantail that flitted around her as she crept forward. and Rena. She drew closer to Te Ngakau's cave and the air grew warmer.

"Where are you?" A movement came from the shadows. She clamped a hand to her racing heart and backed away. as she backed out into the fog which had descended around the pa, shrouding her in a cloak of haze.

Out of the cave walked a tall man, clad only in a feather cloak. His cheeks were dark, etched with moko. Distinctive patterns and swirls marked his upper chest.

"Rena." His familiar smile lit up her world.

Tears welled in her eyes. "Te Ngakau."

"Kāo, my true name is Mātātoa."

Rena stepped forwards and reached up to touch his face. Her fingers spread out over the warm flesh, and she stroked the scarring left by the moko tattooed onto his skin hundreds of years earlier. Long black hair hung down his back.

His hand rose and he touched her cheek. She closed her eyes, relishing the warmth. Her fingers dropped to his chest. Every part of him was warm and a rich brown, like a high-quality rum. In front of her stood a man, a living breathing man.

She looked up at him. "Am I dreaming?"

"No, your love broke the curse."

"How could that be?"

Mātātoa, laughing, pulled her into his chest and rested his chin upon her head.

"You told me you loved me, even as a monster, a taniwha. Your genuine affection broke the curse and made me human, made me feel again. Once I knew you loved me, I realised I loved you too."

Rena lifted her head. "You do?" She gazed up into his chocolate-brown eyes. A light topaz ring encircled each pupil.

"I have loved you for a while Rena, but I tried to deny it. What could I offer you?" He dropped his eyes. "How could a woman love a monster?" A smile curved his lips. "But you did. You loved me."

Rena stood on her tiptoes and brushed his lips with hers. He bent down and pressed their foreheads together.

"How...How did you come back?"

"It had to be, I had to die as the taniwha, so I could be with you as a man." He pulled her tighter, lifted her up and placed his mouth over hers.

"Now, we can be together for as long as it takes." His eyes shone with yearning and he licked his lips. He swept her up in his arms and carried her to the whare puni.

Chapter 23

SUMMERTIME.

The low drone coming from the lake told Rena that Joseph and Sharna were on their way.

"Shall we go to the beach and wait?" Mātātoa said.

She rubbed her belly, feeling nauseous. She wasn't yet showing and not past the early stages. Her mouth felt dry and sticky. While she looked forward to their visits, now wasn't a good time. In another month or two would have been better, but by then their supplies would have run out.

"I'll wait here," Rena said. Mātātoa looked at her, swept her into his arms and laid kisses around her face and neck. She stretched her neck back as far as she could, resisting the urge to throw up.

"We'll be back soon," he said, sighing as he left her. He looked back at her as he left the remains of the pa; the domain of the taniwha. Although Mātātoa was no longer the beast, civilisation was foreign to him, so they had agreed to live at the old pa site. Sharna and Joseph were the only people who knew of their existence.

She'd taken some time to become used to his new name, Mātātoa – Fearless. He explained he'd received the name after rescuing the chieftain's son.

She eased herself down onto the pelt Mātātoa had brought out into the sunshine for her. The early morning sun was already hot, and she was feeling queasier. She reached for her drink bottle and took a long swig of cold water from the underground spring. She picked up the pelt and moved towards the shade of the cave's entrance.

She sighed as she looked back over the spring. She and Mātātoa had spent days celebrating their love, after sending Sharna and Joseph away. It was their first coupling as man and woman that had resulted in this new life that grew within her. She rubbed her flat stomach, knowing that there was life within her.

Mātātoa had wanted a traditional Maori wedding, but those were customs long gone, and Rena parents weren't around for Mātātoa to ask for consent. Instead they agreed to live as a married couple.

As summer approached, Joseph, Sharna and Rena had managed to get Mātātoa as far as Lake Rotoroa, but one look at all the holiday-makers and he'd stopped, raising his hands to his head, shaking. Rena had taken him for a walk along a closed track towards the Sabine Hut, where it was quieter and away from the hustle and bustle of the campers. And even Rena had to agree that after so much isolation, even four people seemed like a crowded mall to her.

She was more than happy to live in the isolated little cove. The pa provided adequate shelter and, with help from Joseph, they had an ample food supply.

The pa had changed a little, modernised.Aa blackened stainless-steel kettle hung over the fire, and a roasting dish sat beside the fire with remnants of last night's meal. Her stomach turned as she thought about the rich wild pork she had enjoyed at the time.

Some food was a little harder to come by, but the cave kept things cold enough for them to store milk and bread.

Mātātoa insisted they keep to a diet of natural fauna and flora for now, and the food hut was full to overflowing with various root stocks, ferns fronds and dried eel and fish. He had allowed beef and chicken meat to be brought in. The chicken, he likened to a weak tasting wood pigeon. Rena had forbidden him to catch or kill any more kereru.

Mātātoa knew that Rena was pregnant before she did, and she'd wondered why he kept giving her a bitter-tasting drink in the first few weeks. Now she wished she had another cup of the foul liquid which, at least, kept the sickness at bay.

Voices and laughter travelled through the bush to where she was sitting. She eased herself to her feet and waited for her head to stop spinning.

Sharna ran up and nearly bowled her over when she threw her arms around Rena.

"Hey gorgeous, isolation suits you."

"So does pregnancy," Rena said, waiting for her friend to react.

Sharna let go. Her mouth dropped open and then her eyes lit up. "Seriously?"

"Yes. Nearly three months."

"Oh my!" Sharna glanced at their surroundings. "Please tell me you don't intend to have the baby here." Her friend hadn't been thrilled when Rena explained she was staying at the pa, for now.

"We'll see what happens," Mātātoa said, coming up beside Rena. He put an arm around her waist. She leaned into him, taking the pressure off her aching back.

"See what happens, my behind!" Sharna, hands on hips, looked more like a mother than a friend.

"Rena needs the best of care, and you ain't going to find that anywhere around here. Now you'll have to move to Nelson."

"We aren't moving to Nelson." Rena's tone was quiet but firm. "We have a place near Wakefield. For Mātātoa, far enough away from people and, for me, close enough to town."

"When did you arrange this?" Sharna looked between the Rena and Mātātoa.

"We've been thinking about it for a while."

"Where did the money come from?"

"I have a savings account, and Mum and Dad offered to help out," Rena winked at Sharna.

Sharna bounced on her feet and threw her arms around Rena again. "You're moving closer? Oh hon, that's fantastic."

Rena eased herself out of her friend's arms. Joseph turned and clapped Mātātoa on the back, offering his congratulations. Mātātoa blushed, and to hide his discomfort he showed her the box of supplies that Sharna and Joseph had brought with them. The smell of fruit filled her nostrils as she glanced into the box, noting oranges, a pineapple, apples and kiwifruit. The thought of some fresh, juicy pineapple was enough for her to forget her morning sickness. For the first time in weeks, she felt well, happy.

And hungry.

The End.

Maori Words and Definition

hangi (ha-gnee) – cooking within a pit in the ground
hei matau (hey ma-toe) - fishhook, greenstone pendant.
horopito (Ho-ro-pee-to) – type of edible fern
kaimoana (ki-mo-a-na) – sea food
Koura (Koo-ra) - crayfish
kete (ke-te) – flax basket or bag
maihi (ma-e-he) - the carved facing boards on the front of the meeting house
Māori (Maa-o-re) – indigenous people of New Zealand
pa – fortified village
pakeha (Par-key-ha) – white person
pikopiko (pee-ko-pee-ko) – fern shoots
poaka puihi (po-a-ka pue-he) - pig
pounamu (Poe -na-mu)– greenstone or New Zealand Jade
taiaha (tie-a-ha) – a spear like weapon
taniwha (tar-nee-far) – a monster or guardian of an area of water or land.
tapu (ta-poo) – curse
tekoteko (te-ko-te-ko)– carve figure on the gable of the meeting house – the figurehead
tuna – (too-na) eel
wahine (wa-he-ney) – woman
wairua (why-ru-a) – dead spirit
whare (Fa-rey) – house / hut
whare nui – (fa-rey noo-ey) big house, the meeting house
whare puni (fa-rey poo-nee) – Sleeping hut

New Zealand Native Birds
tui – Parson bird – Iridescent black green bird with white tuft under chin
korimako - Bellbird – green bird with melodic call
kereru – (ke-re-ru) wood pigeon – large green and white native bird – were popular eating for Māori
piwakawaka (Pee-wa-ka-wa-ka) – fantail

Behind the Story

Normally there is a story behind where tale comes from, but I started to write this story so long ago, (2014) that I really can't remember how the idea originated.

Lake Rotoroa in the Nelson Lakes National Park has always been a magical place for me. A place of mystery and intrigue. And I always wanted to tramp to the Sabine hut, but the track was closed because of tree fall, so unless I went the long way around (Like Rena did) I wouldn't make it to the hut. I did do a lot of research into the area, and used maps to see the topography, so I knew that the track was steep and that with snow melt it would be rather treacherous. Even in the middle of summer some tracks are perpetually wet.

A few years ago, there was a story about a young man who went missing on the lake. He fell out of a boat and was never seen again. It is presumed that the eels in the lake probably got to him. That is how the idea started of a Taniwha in the lake, and eventually the story evolved to become a version of Beauty and the Beast. I guess because it was one of my all-time favourite movies, especially the live action with Emma Watson.

Writing Rob wasn't too hard. I've been with some tremendously horrible men and that is being extremely polite. I have never been physically intimidated by any of them, but I have been in enough situations where I could see how it would happen. And the slow change from being a nice guy to a manipulating chauvinist I have experienced personally, and that was the hard part. But putting Rena through that felt wrong. It feels so wrong for any woman to be in a situation like that, but to have the story make sense, it was a necessary evil. I do realise that some women will struggle with that. And some might think it is just a brush off. Perhaps it is, but Rena is a strong woman, and she wasn't going to put up with that kind of behaviour to her. And why did she run to Lake

Rotoroa? If she went to Nelson, Rob would only track her down. She could 'disappear' when in the bush, her second home.

The idea of Rena going "from the frying pan into the fire" was a concept I wanted to explore. I think that this is where the idea of Beauty and the Beast really came to fruition, I could see how this would work.

But I wanted them to make love, and the only way I could do that was to have the Taniwha change back into a man at will, but that didn't make sense with the 'Beauty and the Beast' theme, so instead, I made it a sweet story, where they fell for each other slowly, and didn't make love until after he changed back to a human.

And this is how Curse of the Taniwha came about.

Gratitude and Beatitudes

Lorna – Elsie Editing Service – Her sharp eye and attention to detail has done wonders for my story.

Kura Carpenter – for her beautiful cover art.

Valetta Sówka – Proofreader extraordinaire, thank you for your help.

To all my fans – (especially **Nicola, Joan, Estelle** and **Viv**) thank you for buying my books. I really appreciate it.

And always -
To my **Mum, my Son, Sheri and My Mr H** – Thank you for your support and encouragement. It means the world to me that you guys believe in me.

Bobba – My guardian angel. From the bottom of my heart, thank you for being there for me.

YOU GUYS ROCK.

Weblinks

Check out the work of those who have assisted me with my writing.

Elsie Editing Service – www.elsieediting.co.nz
Valetta Sówka – www.valettabrenzon.com
Kura Carpenter – www.kuracarpenter.com

Thank you for taking the time to read this book. If you enjoyed it, please leave a review on Goodreads and wherever you purchased this book from.

Who is Catherine Mede?

Catherine Mede lives in Motropolis, in the South Island of New Zealand with her son, a rescue cat Lunar and her partner Mr H. When not writing, Catherine likes to read, draw and work in her garden.

Although having developed a love for writing when she was at High School, it wasn't until she was in her thirties she decided to really get down and dirty with the words in her head.

Romance and Speculative Fiction are the genres Catherine likes to dabble in, because hey, why not? And adding Fantasy elements fulfils her need to create fanciful worlds.

When she was younger, she wrote to escape reality, now she writes it to allow others to enter a world where love has a happily-ever-after ending.

Stalk Catherine Mede on:
Facebook www.facebook.com/Catherine Mede
Pinterest www.pinterest.com/Catherine Mede
Twitter @Catherinemedenz
Instagram @CatherineMede
Website www.catherinemede.com
Email Catherine@catherinemede.com

Cursed Love

A family curse.
A lifetime of grieving.
Jinny Richards' past and future are about to collide.
Will she survive?

At 18, Virginia 'Jinny' Richards was a drug addict who fell in love with Dean Bradford. By 20, Dean was dead. Jinny believes the family curse is to blame, and never wants to fall in love again. She has worked hard to hide her past and now has a job as a successful Insurance Assessor.

Ethan Montgomery lost his wife to breast cancer. He's mourned her for three years and now he's ready to move on. He understands Jinny's pain, but he wants the feisty Jinny and nothing, not even a curse, will stand in his way.

When work throws them together, loving Ethan is the farthest thing from Jinny's mind. He's tardy and egotistical, even if he is good looking and makes her weak at the knees.

Things get further complicated when Steven Bradford turns out to be the client, bringing up the heartache and pain Jinny has carefully buried for eighteen years.

Will she find love a second time around? Or will the family curse claim another victim?

Shards of Ice

Things are heating up on this Ice Planet

Vyvica Karala of the D'Authian Guards had to leave her father behind when the Crown City of Althu was invaded by Ch'ar Barakus. She wants to find her father and is determined to retake the city, with or without the support of the D'Authian Guards.

Kelvaras Mason is a vigilante for hire and has been brought in by the D'Authian Guards to find a leak in their intelligence network. Ch'ar Barakus has also engaged his services; to bring in Vyvica Karala because she has information he needs.

While Vyvica wants to save Elador from Ch'ar, Kelvaras is conflicted in his loyalties.

Vyvica and Kelvaras clash from the moment they meet and set the planet ablaze with their conflicts, yet they can't resist each other.

But both hold dark secrets. If it were known, their lives would be at risk.

Will one of them make the ultimate sacrifice in order for the other to survive?

Running Away

Sometimes the world has a way of making you stop.

Larissa Green has had a rough run. She ditched her boyfriend, quit her job, and lost her flat all in twenty-four hour period. She does what she does best. Larissa turns on her heels to escape her life by doing something totally out of character—going for a tramp.

Harley Orion is an English action movie star, in a toxic relationship. When his girlfriend accuses him of a serious offence, Harley freaks out and runs away to New Zealand until the storm blows over. Anonymity is assured when you stay at an isolated lodge in the beautiful Abel Tasman National Park.

A fateful morning pushes the two together, and they can't deny the chemistry between them, but both are cautious. Harley has been stung by women, Larissa used by men. However they can't stop what happens between them.

Until the true nature of Harley's visit to New Zealand is revealed, destroying Larissa's hope of ending up with her dream man.

But life has a way of making things happen that you least expect.

Finding Amy Archer

Amy Morgan's world is about to come to a crashing halt.

Her son is off to University, her husband has a secret and her best friend has some bad news.

Very bad news

What is a girl to do?

Amy is struggling to find her feet in her ever-collapsing world. But one this is abundantly clear; she now has time to figure out what she wants to do with the rest of her life.

But who is Amy Morgan?
What does she like?
What are her passions?
What does she want to do?

Follow Amy on her path of discovery, learning to love herself and finding her way in a new world without those around her she loves.